STORIES ABOUT TACIT

Stories
About
Tacit

Cecil Bødker

BOOK ONE OF THE WATER FARM TRILOGY

translated from the Danish by
Michael Goldman

… secrets keep people apart
or bind them together…

SPUYTEN DUYVIL
New York City

ACKNOWLEDGMENTS

The first chapter, "Tacit the Bedspread," appeared as "Story of the Week" in The Missing Slate, March, 2016. Sincere appreciation to The Danish Arts Foundation for their financial support towards the translation and publication of this book. Sincere appreciation to Gyldendal Publishing, Copenhagen, for their cooperation in the translation and publication of this book.

THE DANISH ARTS FOUNDATION

Library of Congress Cataloging-in-Publication Data

Names: Bødker, Cecil, author. | Goldman, Michael (Michael Favala), translator.
Title: Stories about Tacit / Cecil Bødker; translated by Michael Goldman.
Other titles: Fortµllinger omkring Tavs. English
Description: New York City : Spuyten Duyvil, 2016. | "Originally published in
    Danish by Arena as Fortµllinger omkring Tavs "1971." | Summary: Follows
    Tacit, a boy whose Granny never speaks of his mother, through his
    childhood and youth when he, now an apprentice blacksmith, helps deliver a
    single woman›s baby.
Identifiers: LCCN 2016020155 | ISBN 9781944682149 pbk | 978-1-944682-76-7 hdc.
Subjects: | CYAC: Identity--Fiction. | Community life--Denmark--Fiction. |
    Grandmothers--Fiction. | Denmark--Fiction.
Classification: LCC PZ7.B635717 Sto 2016 | DDC [Fic]--dc23
LC record available at https://lccn.loc.gov/2016020155

Contents

TACIT THE BEDSPREAD

Tacit didn't know why he had to live with his Granny. At first he didn't even realize he did. Or that it was anything unusual. He had always lived there. It wasn't until other people started asking him where his mother and father were, and why he didn't live with them, that he started to wonder.

Did he even have a mother?

And a father?

And how could anyone else know, when he didn't even know who they were? He marveled at this sudden expansion of his possibilities.It was like he could see farther, and like he couldn't see anything at all. He would have to ask Granny.

Tacit hesitated, because how could Granny know anything about it? No one ever came to her house that he didn't know.

He thought long and hard about all the ladies who came by and entered their house and drank coffee or just stood in the door and chatted. None of them ever said that he had a mother.

Or did they?

Could they have said something like that to Granny when he wasn't listening? When he was out in the sandpile?

He went inside and stared long and questioning at the old woman, while she sat on the kitchen chair, knitting. The aroma of something boiling on the stove filled the room with a nice feeling, but Tacit was too occupied with his own thoughts to notice what it was. He walked over and leaned against Granny's legs which were bent beneath her dark dress.

"Granny?"

She turned her face towards him without pausing in her knitting.

"Granny, is it true that I have a mother?"

"Who says that?"

"Other people."

"Everyone has a mother."

"And a father?"

"Everyone has a father, too."

"Me, too?"

"Aren't you a person?" Granny looked at him over the rim of her narrow glasses.

Tacit thought carefully.

"So do you know her?" he asked.

Granny nodded and her fat bottom lip stuck out, like it always did when he had done something that he wasn't supposed to. Yes, Granny definitely knew his mother.

"And my father too?" he wanted to know.

"No," said Granny and she stood up.

And there was something about the way she said no that made him not want to ask anymore. It wasn't just the bottom lip, even though it was very big now. It was the tone of it.

But he didn't stop thinking.

If Granny knew he had a mother all along, why had she never said anything? He looked at her out of the corner of his eye. She had gotten up and put something on the fire to interrupt him. And he sat down quietly on the floor and started building houses out of the kindling from the firewood box in the corner. Granny knew it the whole time. He was sure of it. The stiff white hairs on her chin twitched while she knitted.

Later he got up carefully and snuck into the cold bedroom, where the hand mirror with the yellowed celluloid rim lay on the dresser's white lace runner. He stared at himself in the mirror for a long time before putting it back again.

Instead of asking more questions he started listening at the door crack when Granny had visitors. Lying motionless on the floor with his ear against the door he followed the conversation, waiting patiently for them to say something about his mother, while the coolness in the dark shiny varnish worked its way into his body. And very gradually he began to realize that something about his situation was different. That was why he lived with Granny.

Silently he got up, snuck out past the guests, and sat down like a well-behaved boy with his sticks and pinecones in the gravel pile where the ladies would pass by. And he observed their bright, righteous faces openly and curiously when they left. They couldn't have known he had been listening. But still they wouldn't look him in the eye, so Tacit was sure. They'd known all along that he had a mother.

But it wasn't until the day they cut his hair and his soft longish locks lay on Granny's kitchen floor that he made the connection. Two neighbor ladies had come to help, and it had taken lots of explaining and persuasion to get him to go along with it. He sat on the kitchen chair in the middle of the floor, and one of the ladies used the scissors while Granny and the other one chatted and chatted to distract him, so he wouldn't run away before they were finished.

They told him that after all, he was a boy, and that boys don't go around with long curls when they get big.

Tacit stared at them dubiously.

"Short hair looks much better," they said.

Tacit had waited as long as he could to climb up on the chair. He knew Granny had long hair. In the evening when she got ready for bed she took the hairpins out of her bun, and a long braid rolled down the back of her nightgown.

3

"But Granny has long hair," he said.

"Granny is a lady," said the woman with the scissors. And Tacit had looked surprised at Granny. He wasn't so sure. A lady?

"You are not a girl," said the other one.

"Granny isn't a lady," he proclaimed.

"She isn't?" said the lady quietly.

"No, because Granny is a Granny."

"You can be both at the same time," said the lady.

Tacit considered this while they tied a dishtowel around his neck. No one had ever cut his hair before.

"Then is my mother a lady too?" he asked.

There was a strange silence in the kitchen, as if no one really knew what to say to that.

"What does her hair look like?" he asked, when no one had answered.

"Your mother?"

"Yes. Is it long?"

"Is was long when she was little, anyway," said the lady with the scissors.

"With curls?"

"It was just like yours."

"How do you know?"

"Because I saw it."

"Where?"

"Right here where we are."

"Did she sit on this same chair?"

"I'm sure she did."

"And got her hair cut with these scissors?"

"No, because she was a girl."

Tacit sat thinking for a while and felt the cold of the scissors against the skin on the back of his neck.

"Why did she sit here in this chair?" he asked.

"Because she was Granny's little girl back then," the woman quickly answered.

It got quiet again.

"Is she still?"

"Sure, but now she's grown up."

One long lock after another fell on the floor and the lady with the scissors slowly made her way around the chair.

"Why doesn't she ever come over?" asked Tacit.

"I guess because she lives so far away."

The sound of the scissors filled the room. Granny had had them sharpened for the occasion. And when he was all done she brought the mirror for him to look in. And he sat a long while gazing at his new appearance, trying to recognize himself.

"See how nice you look," said the ladies. "You look much nicer now."

Tacit stayed sitting out in the kitchen, while the others went into the living room with coffee and clinking coffee cups. It was strange. They said that his mother had hair like him when she was little. Granny had swept his hair into a little pile in the corner so no one would step in it and track it into the living room. And Tacit let himself slide down onto the floor with the mirror in his hand. The scissors were still on the table. He traded them for the mirror. Then he collected some of the hair from the pile and tried cutting it.

It didn't hurt at all. Not even if he took a big clump. He couldn't feel anything, even though it was his own hair. It just floated down to the kitchen floor again in tiny pieces.

When there were no curls left, he tried cutting the dishrag, but that was hard. Too fat and lumpy. And it was wet. You couldn't cut wet things. The tea towel was much easier. That made nice long strips. But it wasn't like hair. Hair was more fun. He tried cutting more of the pile on the floor, but the tiny pieces slipped from his fingers. It wasn't much of a pile anymore.

Over in front of the heater, Granny's fat tomcat was lying with its paws under its belly and its nose down on the warm tiles.

He paused and looked at it before he tried.

But that didn't work either. It scratched him and ran off with a little blood on its ear. Tacit was disappointed. If everyone says that you look better with your hair cut, and that you should sit still while it's being done, why did it leave? Why didn't the kitty have to look nice when *he* had to?

He pushed open the living room door slightly, with the scissors behind his back. They grinned at him from their coffee cups to convince him that he still looked nice with short hair. And he walked past their voices and smiles into the bedroom, where Granny's white bedspread lay across the big bed with the fringes hanging down to the floor on both sides.

The fringes were long and delicate. Tacit fingered them gently before he went to work. This time he knew he got it right. The fringes fell just as his hair had done, collecting in little curls on the floor. He worked diligently, but it took longer than he'd figured and the big scissors hurt his fingers more than he'd expected. But the ladies had said that you couldn't just cut one side. It had to be even. So he persevered until he had made it all the way around and there was not a single fringe remaining.

Then he stepped back from the bed and cocked his head to the side just like the ladies had done. And his delight over the bedspread's new appearance was no less than the ladies' delight when they saw his haircut.

They had said that he looked a lot older.

The bedspread did too, thought Tacit. There were some

places where they had old bedspreads on their beds, and the fringes were almost completely worn off. He was as good at cutting as the ladies. Full of pride he opened the door to the living room and asked them to come in and see how nice it looked.

Three pairs of eyes anxiously noticed the scissors at his side. It grew quiet. Then his world tumbled down around him. Both visiting ladies clasped their hands together and spouted off about lots of things that he had never heard before. There was something about his mother and something about his father, and a lot about what ever would become of him.

But why wasn't it just as good to cut the fringe off the bedspread as it was to cut his hair? They had all said that it wasn't proper to have it hanging there.

Granny took the scissors out of his hand, but to the ladies' disappointment, she didn't hit him. She didn't even yell at him. Instead, she led the boy in front of her, back into the bedroom and laid him down across the big bed with his head hanging over the edge.

And she told him that he could just keep lying there.

Inside the boy's eyes she was standing on her head. It looked funny. The ladies in the doorway were standing on their heads too. "You should spank him," they said. "If he was one of our ... "

Tacit shivered at the thought. It was a good thing he was Granny's.

"Now just keep lying there until I come back," she said. And Tacit could see by her lower lip that she meant it. She nudged the ladies back into the living room and shut the door.

But he could still hear what they said. And he could also hear that they drank more coffee.

"Why didn't you box his ears?" asked the one that had cut

7

his hair. It sounded like she was angry with Granny.

"It wouldn't work," said Granny. "He had to be taken."

That made Tacit jump. Be taken? Who was going to take him? Was he supposed to lie here so someone could come and take him?

"Hitting doesn't work," said Granny.

"No, it must be that blood," said the other one pointedly.

Tacit stiffened. Did they find out about that too? That he had cut the cat's ear?

"But that's what we've said all along," said the lady. "It will never work out. But it's your own fault."

"If you think your Ephraim is any prettier, then you're wrong," said Granny in the tone she used when she didn't want to hear about something anymore. Then they started to talk about houseplants.

Prettier how? thought Tacit. He didn't think Ephraim was pretty at all. His ears stuck out. But he had already had short hair for a long time. He forgot about the cat, and how he had cut it, and he just lay there looking up at the ceiling, waiting for Granny to come back like she had said. When he bent his head back all the way he could see the cut-off fringes down on the floor. They lay there and hadn't been swept together in a pile yet like the hair in the kitchen.

His neck was getting tired. Why didn't she come back like she said, since they were only sitting there, talking. He could hear that they weren't drinking coffee now. They were talking about someone named Joanna.

Tacit didn't know anyone named Joanna. He wasn't really interested. He just wished that Granny would come and say that he could go out and play now.

He twisted himself around so he could see the branches outside the window. In the living room the ladies were finally getting ready to leave and go home. And he could hear how

Granny followed them out through the utility room as usual. Now she had to come.

But Granny just started to clean up the coffee dishes.

After Tacit had lain there for a very long time, he went out and asked what happened to her.

"Why aren't you coming?"

"I'm not going to bed yet," said Granny, surprised. "It's the middle of the day. I'll come when I go to sleep."

"But why do I have to keep lying in there?" His voice was a little agitated.

"Because you are a bedspread," said Granny.

Tacit wrinkled his brow. Her bottom lip wasn't sticking out so much.

"But a boy can't be a bedspread," he answered.

"Of course he can," Granny assured him in all seriousness. "If a bedspread can be a boy then a boy can be a bedspread too."

Tacit stood there thinking.

"But I don't think a bedspread can be a boy either," he said.

"Are you sure about that?"

Tacit nodded enthusiastically.

"Then why did you cut its hair?"

Granny didn't stop carrying in cups and dishes and washing them. She walked back and forth between the living room and the kitchen and spoke as if didn't matter to her one bit who was the bedspread on her bed.

"Do I have to lie there until all the fringes are grown out again," asked Tacit anxiously.

That would take a long time, he thought. Fringes probably didn't grow very fast. At any rate, he didn't think they had grown any longer as far back as he could remember.

"Well that depends on whether or not we can agree on

who's going to be a boy and who's going to be a bedspread here in this house," said Granny.

"You could also be a dish towel and hang up on the nail," she added, holding some shreds of a towel up in the air. "I think I could use something to dry the cups with."

Tacit glanced at the nail by the heater, and Granny swept the pile of hair together on the tiles one more time. She picked up some of it and looked at it. For a long time, thought Tacit.

EPHRAIM'S EARLOBE

Every time he happened to look at the spot where Ephraim's earlobe should have been, it made him think about how it had looked lying in the road, like a little, pale, flat stone. There hadn't been a trace of red on it. That was because he had kept it in his mouth for so long before he spit it out.

It was just lying there, and a little bit of sand had gotten on it since it was damp. But by then Ephraim was already way down the road, bawling at the top of his lungs, and with blood running down his neck.

No one had picked it up.

Sometimes he wondered if maybe someone found it later, or if it was just left there for carts to run over. Or if maybe it had gotten kicked into the roadside ditch, or eaten by a dog.

Anything could happen to an earlobe just lying there, all alone like that. And no one ever mentioned that they had seen it. Maybe they thought that he had eaten it, but he hadn't. He had spit it out on the road.

Every time he saw Ephraim he stared at the spot where it had been. The sore had healed long ago, and now there was a strange, little bumpy thing there at the bottom of his ear. Not that it was so noticeable, unless you knew about it beforehand, and about what had happened. But if you looked, you could tell that ear was very different from the one on the other side of his head.

He stared at that ear too, especially the earlobe. It had been just like that.

But it didn't feel strange at all, having it in his mouth. Once in a while one of the others asked him if it had been disgusting, but he didn't think so.

And besides, Ephraim could have just stayed away.

No one had told Ephraim to show up and be annoying and everything, just because he was there in the roadside ditch, without even really admitting to himself what he was there for.

Why did Ephraim have to plant himself there, asking questions. He could have just kept on walking and kept his mouth shut.

Or stayed home.

There was no law against sitting in the ditch, or any other ditch for that matter. And he wasn't siting there because he knew Camilla was going to pass by, not at all, and there was no law against looking for wild strawberries either.

Of course it didn't bother him at first when Ephraim thought he was collecting ant eggs, since he had pulled up so many clumps of grass. It wasn't that, but it was the way he had said it, and the way his dumb, watery eyes had scanned the ground of the ditch. And that he just stood there.

As if he also knew that Camilla was going to pass by.

And when that wasn't even why he was sitting there. No one had ever told Ephraim that *he* couldn't play with her or walk with her or anything. It was only himself. Her mother never liked him, and the more he played with her, the more mad her mother got.

It was like there was something wrong with taking Camilla to the secret places in the woods or down to the bog. He knew what her mother was so afraid of. But it wasn't like that at all.

And he could still feel what it was like, how her mother had stood there kneading the dough with her stubby, angry hands while she told him that Camilla wasn't coming out. That Camilla had to help in the house, that she was big now, and that she couldn't always just be out roaming around.

He had stared at her hands.

It looked like she was really mad at the dough, as if it had done something to her. And he didn't say a word, but just kept looking at her. The way her shoes were splitting a bit at the seams, the way her hair stuck out in thin wisps from under her headscarf. He looked until she noticed it and showed her irritation.

"What are you staring at, boy?"

And how he had infused himself with held back amusement, and acted like he was in high spirits so she wouldn't know how he felt.

And how he had just turned around and left.

After that he always stared intently at her any time he happened to see her, just because he knew she didn't like it. The way she hoed sugar beets, the way she lifted her head when he approached, and the way she immediately acted as if she hadn't seen him. The way her slip showed in the front. And how her hair always came out from under her headscarf no matter how tightly she tied it.

The ugly rubber boots with the broken heels.

His eyes were wide open, filled with what they observed, and he was sure that she could feel it. It was her fault that Ephraim had to lose his earlobe. In any case, just as much as it was Ephraim's own fault.

Every time he saw the spot where it was missing, he thought about the ditch out by the road and how he had been sitting halfway down in it when he saw Ephraim come clomping in a pair of adult clogs. At the time he couldn't have known what was going to happen. He just felt his muscles tighten with irritation at the sight of him.

Not because he had anything against him otherwise. But why was Ephraim walking by just when he was sitting in the ditch not wanting to be seen, with no chance of escaping. No one was supposed to know he was there.

And what could he do except slip down to the bottom and act like he didn't care? He wasn't going to let Ephraim think he was afraid of him.

But it was almost like getting caught in a trap.

And it wasn't any better with Ephraim parading around in a pair of clogs that weren't even his. They were too big, probably his father's.

He kept sitting completely still, down in the ditch, without so much as looking up at the road, even though Ephraim was trying really hard to make himself noticed.

At the same time he happened to think that Camilla might have taken another way home to avoid him. And he started to hate her almost as much as he hated her mother.

Ephraim came to a stop, and with an insinuating grin asked why he was down there.

"No reason."

The response was dismissive. Ephraim knew very well that sometimes there were strawberries there.

"Are you collecting ant eggs?" Ephraim wanted to know, even though he had heard that Granny didn't have pheasant chicks any more.

His body curled up down in the ditch.

"None of your business."

What else could he say? But Ephraim didn't get it. Not why the grass was pulled up in clumps or that he should keep on walking. He just stood there gawking and said, "What's going on?" like he was talking to a crazy person. And he just stood there staring, his mouth open, even though there was nothing to stare at.

"What's your problem? Get lost. Go."

But that was when Ephraim planted himself there in his stupid clogs and starting acting all annoying.

"Not until you tell me why you're sitting there," he said.

And it didn't help at all to stare at him furiously. Or to say, "Shut up and get lost," And things like that.

Ephraim just answered, "Hey, you don't own the road."

And, "I haven't done anything to you."

And, "Who the hell are you? You think you get to decide who gets to walk along the road?"

And the whole time Ephraim just stood there trying to find out what he was doing down there in the ditch and why so many clumps of grass were pulled up. But he wasn't going to let Ephraim know what it was like, when you just sit there in a place like that, not really knowing why you are there, or what you would say if she suddenly came by.

"Don't you think I know that you're sitting there waiting for a girl?" said Ephraim, full of contempt, up on the road.

Afterwards he couldn't remember getting out of the ditch. He didn't really notice how it happened. Only that he violently opened his scrunched body, was suddenly up on the road, butting his head into Ephraim's gut, so Ephraim got the wind knocked out of him. He felt Ephraim bend in half from the impact.

Ephraim was bigger and heavier, but he wasn't very fast. And this particular, strange feeling of being completely white inside, that had infused him while he sat down in the ditch, made it easy for him to topple Ephraim onto the road and throw himself on top.

It was while they were lying there like that, kicking up dust and taking turns groaning with effort, that they heard her say something right next to them.

"You're in the way," she said, not daring to go by, for fear of getting kicked.

They hadn't heard her coming, and who could say how long she had been standing there, looking at them. And that was about the worst thing that could have happened, because now Ephraim would think that he had been right all along, even though he was on the bottom. What else could they do but get up, brush off the worst of the dirt from their clothes, and wait for her to go by.

But Camilla wouldn't go past. Instead she asked, "Why are you fighting?"

There really wasn't any way to answer that, and it was a little while before he pulled himself together enough to take a good look at her. Higher than just her feet.

She had braids.

It was the first time he had seen her like that, and he froze at the sight. Her hair usually hung loosely down her back.

Her mother had done it. And she wasn't the same Camilla anymore. She seemed completely different and much older. How could he even think of talking to her when she looked like that.

He had wiped his mouth on his sleeve. His lip was bleeding.

Ephraim's clogs were still lying there where he had kicked them off. And Camilla had just stood there waiting.

But then Ephraim started saying all these things in this particular voice that was oozing with how he knew everything. That he knew all along it was a girl, that it was her he had been sitting there waiting for, and that they were boyfriend and girlfriend, and all kinds of things.

They were not boyfriend and girlfriend. There was nothing else he could do but just ram him in the stomach again, but this time Ephraim was more prepared, and when he realized that he couldn't hold Ephraim down he bit his arm. That took the know-it-all tone out of Ephraim's voice.

"Goddammit," Ephraim roared, flipping him from his body. "That's nasty! You fight like a dog!"

So he had to jump on him again.

But it wasn't until after they had tangled together on the road for a while, and Ephraim had tried to hit him in the head with one of the clogs, that he really bit down hard.

And that was when he got something in his mouth.

Was it a piece of Ephraim?

Ephraim worked himself loose, howling, got up and screamed, "You bastard!" holding his ear while blood ran down his neck.

He lie on the ground, feeling with his tongue what it was he had in his mouth. A piece of Ephraim, he thought.

And he remembered how Camilla had held both her hands on her cheeks as if a murder had been committed right there in the middle of the road in front of her.

"What is wrong with you," she had whispered. "That was his ear."

That was when he got up and spit the earlobe in the direction of its owner who already was on his way home.

"I fight like a dog," he had answered and felt a strange, inward pride. For a second he thought that he could cope with her braids. If he didn't look directly at her, anyway.

"You forgot your clogs!" he yelled towards Ephraim.

And Ephraim had turned around, with his hand full of blood, before running farther away.

"What did he do?" asked Camilla.

"Nothing," he mumbled. She was too unfamiliar to just talk with. And definitely not about that.

"Well, then what were you fighting for?"

"Nothing."

He could tell that it sounded dumb, that he didn't have any real answer, but there was nothing else he could say.

Then he had just sat down in the ditch again, because he didn't know what else he should do. That's where he had been sitting before. Now he didn't know how he was going to get away from there. He would have to wait until Camilla had left.

But she didn't go. She just stayed there standing up on the road waiting for an explanation for what had happened.

Then suddenly she jumped down and sat next to him, with her braids and her changed appearance, and a fever coursed through him.

Quietly, she said, "It's okay to tell me why you were fighting."

"It wasn't for anything, like I said."

Saying it like that made him feel like he was cutting into his own flesh.

"You bit off his ear."

"Not all of it."

He had never touched a braid except for Granny's. Camilla had two. They looked heavy, with her sitting there bent forward a little, poking at the ground with a stick. He was embarrassed about having pulled up the grass like that. Why wouldn't she say that Ephraim was a jerk and that she couldn't care less what he had said?

"Don't you have to go home?" he had asked.

She didn't answer, but kept sitting there like she was waiting for them to talk like they always had done before, before her mother said that they couldn't be together anymore.

"You could have gone with Ephraim," he continued, and heard how mean it sounded. Still he had to keep on. His inner torment from sitting with her like that was more than he could bear.

"You could have carried his clogs," he said, "and his earlobe. He forgot that too."

Her smooth tan arms emerged from her dress way up at her shoulders, and he had never noticed before how they looked. Her skin was different than his. Everything on her was different because he hadn't seen her for so long. He could have bit her hand if he'd dared, sunk his teeth deep into her arm and sucked some of her blood. That would have helped.

Instead, he said, "Don't you need to go home and help your mother? Don't you need to make yourself useful, now that you've gotten so big?"

His voice was mocking.

"Why don't you leave?"

She got up, and her arms hung down on both sides of her body. Without a word she started to walk away very slowly.

Her back looked as if someone had hit her.

And she didn't turn around. Not even once did she turn and look back, not even when he yelled that she had forgotten Ephraim's clogs.

He stood in the road watching her go. And when she was far away, he had taken Ephraim's clogs and smashed them down onto the roadway as hard as he could. But they didn't break. They were too big and had lots of metal fasteners.

And that was when he happened to see the earlobe lying there by itself where he had spit it out. It had a little gray sand around the edge.

THE WATER FARM

In a deep hollow beside the road, in an out-of-the-way corner of the parish, there was an old red farmhouse. Granny's voice got big and heavy when she spoke about it. He lived there. They called him "the murderer," and they tried not to mention him when there were children present.

The farmhouse was quite old. And it wasn't that the land had sunken with it, even though it might look like that. It was built down there, people said. No one knew by whom anymore, and now it stood there with the whole wide world sloping down towards its thin gray roof.

Tacit had walked by it before and had looked down on it from the road up on the rim. The area was so remote that the roadway was getting green from lack of traffic. Down in the hollow a swampy channel emerged from behind the farm out towards the beach. In landward storms you could hear the ocean rumbling out at the cliffs.

"Why is he called the murderer?" asked Tacit.

Granny's fat bottom lip slid forward ominously and she didn't answer.

"Did he murder someone?"

"That's what people say."

"Is it true?"

"You can't say for sure when you don't really know."

"But does everyone say that?"

"Yes, everyone says that."

"Shouldn't he go to jail?"

Tacit thought of the jails he had read about and about the farm out there that he had seen from above.

"He was in jail," said Granny.

"Then he must have killed someone."

"I can't say."

"Do you know who it was?"

"I'm pretty sure it was another man, a neighbor."

Tacit sighed, relieved. Just imagine if the murderer had been in jail for nothing. And had to live all alone on that farm for no reason.

"Where did he do it? There's no neighbors way out there. So how could he kill a neighbor?"

"He's not from around here," said Granny. "It didn't even happen here. He must have had a house someplace else.'

"Then why does he live here?"

"Because no other place would have him. And then one day he came by here and the Water Farm was vacant."

"Was it always like that?"

"Not always, but for a long time. A very long time. The people who owned it had to abandon it."

A feeling of loneliness on behalf of the old farm came over Tacit, and the sight of people crawling up the steep slope to the road got stuck in his head.

"It was because the farmyard and all around was flooded," continued Granny, "And they couldn't get it to go down again."

Up on the slope a crowd of people turned and saw how the sky and the walls were mirrored in the polished lake around the buildings.

"It was the thaw," said Granny. "It flowed in through the cattle house. In one door and out through the other. They had to go out there at night with brooms and sticks to keep the cows from laying down in it. All the floors were flooded.

The pigs, too, which either drowned or died of pneumonia. But they saved the cows."

"What about inside the house?"

"Everything was flooded," said Granny. And everything they had in the barn was ruined."

"So they left with the cows?"

Granny nodded.

Tacit understood. He could see them pulling the tired, wet cows behind them, up over the incline and disappearing.

"What about the children?"

"Yes, the children, too," said Granny. "You always take the children with you when you move."

Boys and girls his age turned and looked back on their flooded home. Their beds, he thought.

"And their dogs and cats," he said.

"I don't know," said Granny.

"And all the chickens," said Tacit, thinking about Granny's henhouse.

"I don't know," said Granny. "I never heard about any chickens."

"Only the cows?"

"Yes, only about the cows."

"And the pigs?"

"All the pigs died."

"What about the fields?" asked Tacit. "They couldn't take them with them, could they?"

"The neighbors took them over."

Tacit nodded. That sounded reasonable. And he saw the dense fields of grass on the flat ground around the hollow glide away from the abandoned farm and set out into the landscape to relocate themselves beside other better situated properties.

"They split them up among themselves," explained Granny.

"And the chickens?" asked Tacit.

"Yes, they probably got them, too."

"And all the cats."

"Yes," said Granny, "If you insist. But I think the cats stayed where they were."

"Did they drown?"

"They lived up in the attic. There wasn't any water up there."

"And the dog?"

"You always take a dog with you when you move to a new place," said Granny.

Out on the horizon the people herded their cows along and got smaller and smaller. And along with their dog they left the old farm behind.

Tacit sat completely still and felt how empty it had become. How the water had kept lapping against the foundation and sneaking inside through the crack under the door.

"Then the man came and lived there," he said.

"No. First it was empty for a long time."

"Why?"

"No one wanted to live on a farm that was so badly situated and that had no land with it anymore. There was just the house and the hillsides."

"And then the man came and lived there?" asked Tacit.

"Yes," said Granny, "Then one day he came."

"Why doesn't anyone ever visit him?"

"They don't want to. People pretend that he's not there."

"Are they afraid of him?"

" Yes, that's probably why."

"Do you think he's going to kill more people?"

"Definitely not. He's an old man now. I'm sure he doesn't want to go back to jail."

"I want to go visit him."

"And what if he doesn't want you to?"

"When no one else ever does?"

"Well, you know he never goes out anywhere, either. Anyway you're too little."

"I've been over there and I saw the roof and nothing happened."

"You heard what I said."

Tacit didn't answer, but drifted outside with his hands in his pockets, waiting for Granny to forget what they had talked about. Then he left to have another look at that farm. He wasn't too little. He was old enough to decide. And there was something wonderfully tempting about a place where things happened. Where plain water could make people move away. He thought that was interesting. And where a murderer lived who might have even killed a man, who in any case was in prison for it a long time. And that was definitely true, even though Granny didn't like talking about it.

This needed investigating. Thirteen is not too little.

But he stayed standing up by the road, at the top of the incline, when he had gotten far enough to look down onto the old gray roof. Not because he was afraid, but it couldn't do any harm just to wait around a little, and see if anything happened, see if there was anyone down there.

There wasn't.

Tacit didn't see anyone anyway, The only thing that came up from the hollow was the strange feeling of abandonment that he had felt before. The buildings cowered as if they didn't want to draw attention to themselves. Even the chimneys seemed shy and subdued, scrawny and wrinkled as if they didn't get enough to eat, or had a deep-seated illness. They couldn't even give off smoke.

It's probably from all that water they had, thought Tacit. Their bases are probably rotted away from all the water.

Ruined. But they were still standing upright like dead treetrunks from their spot on the property, jutting up through the roof with no connection to the rest of the surrounding house.

Tacit had seen trees like that in a lake deep in the woods. They stood with black trunks and old knotty branches, without a trace of green, far out in the water. They had grown up and been real trees once, but now they were like ghosts standing there, waiting for the day that a storm would topple them, just like one day a storm would topple the old farmhouse's shriveled chimneys down into the farmyard.

The thatch on the roof was worn all the way down to the string it was tied with. If it weren't for the fact that the buildings were so low in the landscape and sheltered from the wind by the road, the roof would long ago have been worn down to the naked rafters. No one would have tried to prevent it. No one was going to come and lay on a new sheaf if there was a hole. Or would he — the man that lived there?

Tacit made his way farther down the incline and discovered what must have been the old wagon track to the farm. It hadn't been driven on in years. It was completely green and overgrown, but still led downwards.

He made it down so far that he could see an old timber sled at the entrance to the barn. It was green with age, and stinging nettles grew up through it, anchoring it to the spot. He didn't go any closer.

Instead he stared with amazement at the farthest chimney. The hairs on his neck stood up. There was smoke coming out of it, a hesitant, nearly transparent smoke, a delicate rippling that dissolved and disappeared. Tacit retreated backwards up the slope, without taking his eyes off of the smoke. And the chimney didn't stop. It kept putting out smoke and he was sure he wasn't imagining it. The house was breathing on him like a corpse can exhale an old breath, and his hands helped him back his way out, up the incline. He didn't dare turn his back on it.

What could happen then?

Who would be following him up the incline when he turned back around?

The murderer?

Or the people with the wet cows?

Or the water? Would the water splash up and grab for his legs? He didn't know what to think. He didn't stop until he was back on the road, where he sniffed down towards the hollow like an unfamiliar dog.

It was regular wood smoke.

Relieved, he walked home trying to pretend that he hadn't been anywhere.

"What did he say to you?" asked Granny.

"Nothing," said Tacit.

"Do you think he saw you? Did you go down there?"

"There was smoke coming out of one of the chimneys," said Tacit.

"Well, okay." said Granny. And Tacit felt it again on the back of his neck.

"But there wasn't any water," he continued, as if it had just occurred to him how dry it had looked.

"That could be," said Granny.

"Do you think it could come back?"

She looked at him a while, considering this.

Finally she said, "No one knows".

HORSE OR HEN

"Hen or rooster?" he asked, closing his fingers around a grass stem at the road edge.

"Hen," said Camilla.

"Rooster," said Tacit, feeling how the seeds compressed together in his grip as he pulled up. He opened his hand and looked.

"Hen," Camilla determined and laughed.

He threw the seeds at her and tried again, with the same result.

"It's hen-day today," she laughed, dancing in front of him down the road.

"No, it's something much more dangerous," said Tacit, to get back at her.

She turned around and became serious.

"Why won't you tell me where we're going?" she wanted to know.

"Because then you'll run away."

"No I won't. You always think I'm afraid of everything. Are we going to borrow a boat — is that it?"

Camilla wasn't so crazy about "borrowing" boats out on the beach, and she was terrified when they got out so far that she couldn't see the bottom, even though she didn't want to admit it.

"No," said Tacit knowingly.

"But we're almost all the way to the beach."

"We're not going out on a boat."

He took her hand and pulled her along down the steep incline towards the old vacant farm. Today was the day he was going to see what it was like.

Camilla resisted until they were all the way down. Then she kept close to him. They paused at the timber sled at the gable. Grass and weeds were growing between the cobblestones in the farmyard. Some places they were shorter then others, as if they had been worn down. The black windowpanes of the farmhouse stared collectively outwards. There were no curtains.

Tacit crossed the farmyard, followed closely on his heels by Camilla, and tried the front door.

"No." She anxiously grabbed his arm. "Don't do that."

The door was locked.

Or nailed shut from the inside, or something like that. Maybe there were boards across it.

Or maybe it hadn't been used in so long, that it was stuck shut permanently. The bottom was rotted.

"We have to at least look in," said Tacit and he put his hands up around his eyes and his forehead against the cold glass in the adjacent window. " At least we have to see what the rooms look like."

Inside was empty space where wallpaper hung loosely from the walls and the floors were so soft and rotten that you could see the underlying dirt in places.

The house was very old and long. Quietly they moved from window to window observing all the different rooms and all the open or closed doors in between. The emptiness on the inside followed them quietly. No one lived here.

At the gable they turned the corner and entered a different tiny courtyard through a very narrow passage with a half-open wooden gate. The cattle house and the farmhouse nearly touched one another at this spot. The rotten wood over the plank gate tied them together.

Here they stopped. Here was the water.

As soon as he saw it, Tacit knew that this was the water which back then had driven the inhabitants away. It wasn't a flood anymore, just a spring. An iron pipe, thick as an arm, was hammered directly into the ground. It stood there a bit crooked, crusted over with rust, leaning over a couple of boulders. And up through the pipe came a constant stream of murmuring spring water. There was no pump; no one had to do anything to make it come out. It just came streaming out of the pipe, splashing down into a carved stone trough. The sound of falling water filled with coolness the little courtyard between the two gables and the hill. Here was a place you could stand for a long time without noticing it, a place where time relaxed and slowed down. Tacit followed the water with his eyes from the watering trough, which was about as long as a man, out through the drain opening in the opposite end. From there a stone gutter carried it to behind the cattle house, and there the nettles closed over it protectively. Only the sound remained in the little courtyard.

They used to water the cows here back then, thought Tacit. They stood here around the trough with their muzzles down in the coolness. That was before the water sought out the thirsty livestock itself, in the cattle house stalls.

The door in the farmhouse gable was shut from the outside with a hasp. Tacit went over and lifted it, and Camilla grabbed his shirt as if in warning. "Remember who lived here," she said.

"No one lives here," said Tacit, pulling her with him into the deteriorating house. "You can see it's totally empty."

Silent as shadows they made their way through rooms where the decay seemed to advance inward through the walls and up through the floor. Dark soil spread in fan patterns from the places where the walls had rotted.

Camilla pointed at tracks in the spreading dirt.

"Animals are getting in," she whispered.

"It's probably rats," he said. "But they only come out at night."

A rat poked up halfway and then disappeared when it saw them. Tacit shrugged. Blades of grass, long and blonde as hair, grew in cracks in the wall, never to return to the sun and wind. He felt something like sadness upon seeing them.

"I'm getting out of here," whispered Camilla, pulling him with her.

They wandered out the long way, back through the house. The water from the bowels of the earth lay there outside in a large clear semicircle around the iron pipe, fitting aptly with the dead house. No one lived here. The water lived here. The man people called "the murderer" must be something they made up. Tacit stuck his head up to the water stream and drank. It was ice cold and he felt his skin harden and his eyes wither. He thought about the people who had fled. They were real.

"Look," yelled Camilla suddenly, wavering between laughter and fear.

Tacit pulled back his face, water dripping from his forehead, chin and nose.

"What is it?"

He dried his stiffened skin on his sleeve but couldn't see anything. The cold had penetrated his eyes and blinded him.

"I can't see a thing. I'm blind as a bat," he said.

"A fish," said Camilla.

The surprise in her voice helped the blood return to his face and eyes, and skeptically he looked where she was pointing. The bottom of the trough was darkened by fallen leaves from the autumn.

He spotted the nearly motionless fish in the water current with its snout pointed up towards the spring pipe.

"Do you think it came out of the pipe?" whispered Camilla uneasily when her surprise had subsided. Tacit looked at the coarse crusty pipe. Only if it had hit it in the face, he thought. He shook his head, and Camilla looked anxiously around the little courtyard between the two gables, but there was nothing there but the hill behind an old tool shed.

"Don't you think we'd better go?" she mumbled. She didn't like the fact that a fish had suddenly appeared. What if that was what lived here?

Tacit stood in the midst of the resonance of the water, and could not tear himself away from the grayish-black living thing in the stone trough. Was that it's soul?

The water's soul?

Or the farm's?

Or was it maybe the murderer who had turned himself into a fish?

He caught a couple of flies and dropped them into the continuously streaming water to demonstrate his good intentions to the creature. But the fish didn't stir, and the water carried the flies indifferently out through the drain opening and down into the gutter.

What if it *had* come out of the pipe?

Or what if it had been in the trough the whole time since the big flood? Could it be that the water covering the farmyard was once full of fish? And that there were fish in the cattle house those nights when the water was flowing in there?

Tacit turned away from the trough and walked in to where the cows had been. But it was dry and clean and the cow halters hung silently and empty from the worn down planking in the stalls. There was something expectant in the way they hung there. The dilapidation here was different than in the farmhouse rooms. It was as if this building was still waiting for the cows to come back and fill the large low space with sounds of rumination and a sweet warm smell.

Tacit leaned in and snuck a look over the bricked-up edge of the pig pen. But there were no dead pigs—and no dead fish.

In the farthest stall towards the entry doors there was a bit of hay scraped together in a corner and a long dog chain led out though a half open door. Deep wear marks down in the door jamb told of a long and loyal service, scars from dogs' lives in eternal captivity, dog after dog after dog keeping out unbidden guests. Now only the empty chain was left to guard the dead farm.

But they took the dog with them when they left. Or did they? There was no collar on the end of the chain.

Big dogs, thought Tacit. Giant dogs made mean by always keeping them tied up.

Would they take a dog like that with them?

How long could it swim on the end of the chain before it drowned? He closed his fingers around the chain but it was cold.

Camilla came over beside him and looked up at the entry roof, where long fingers of light drilled down through the thatch, pointing at languid cobweb cloths, darkened frocks and veils that swayed between the joists, thick as wool from years of solitude.

While they stood there with upturned faces, a rumbling blow shook the ground beneath them, resounding all through the empty buildings, and made them jump startled together.

The murderer, they both thought. Was he coming?

They listened for a while with their mouths open, but the sound didn't come back.

"What do you think that was," mumbled Tacit, looking outside where an old road led away through the ravine. The water from the spring pipe flowed around and behind the cattle house, collecting in a little pond beside the road. There was nothing moving.

He walked out to the farmyard again with Camilla reluctantly following after him. "Just need to look," he said. "Have to see what it was."

At this end of the structure there was a window and a door. The farmhand's quarters, thought Tacit, and he was going to pass by it. But something moved on the other side of the window. They both saw it at the same time, and Camilla put her hand over her mouth in alarm. The door was closed from the outside with a hook above and another one farther down.

It was a horse.

Their feet were anchored to the spot. Their bodies were heavy and fixed as pillars. There was a horse standing there, looking at them through the window. Yellow dun with relaxed, interested eyes. Camilla bit her hand to keep from screaming. Tacit and the horse looked at one another.

What was it doing there—in the farmhand's quarters—when there was a real horse barn with an outside entrance? He looked at the door latches. It stood inside so serenely, without making the least effort to escape. It seemed tame. He considered for a while. The panes were rather small and dirty, and the head on the other side seemed large. It was a real horse, that much he was sure of, with dark, vibrant eyes. He didn't open the door.

But the abandoned spirit of the entire farm collected itself in the horse's long sorrowful head. All the vacant rooms stared out at him through the horse's quiet gaze. It had resigned itself to standing there.

For a second it occurred to him that they had forgotten it when they left with the cows, so he shook his head at himself. He searched his pockets, but didn't have anything to give to it.

"I want to go home," said Camilla, pulling him along with her. " I don't want to be here anymore. It's too creepy."

Tacit let himself be dragged away reluctantly. The fish didn't want his flies either. It probably wouldn't have worked even if he had had some bread in his pocket.

"Come on," said Camilla impatiently.

"We can go out by the water and crawl up," he suggested.

Camilla agreed. She felt a little more comfortable there, so it didn't bother her that Tacit took another look at the fish. Curious, she tiptoed over and stared in through the dirty window in the crooked tool shed. Outhouse, she thought, or shovels and spades and things like that. It was dark inside and it took a little while before she could make out anything. Then she jumped backwards.

"There's someone in there," she gasped.

Tacit looked up from the fish doubtfully.

"It's the glass," he said. "It's your reflection."

"Then come see—if you're not too scared," said Camilla.

Her voice was hardened with fear. And inside the shed there really was some kind of thing crouched on a partition. A big sphere, whatever that could be. A giant cat? One of them that had lived in the attic where there was no water and where all the mice probably escaped to as well. Granny had said that people didn't take cats with them.

Camilla was already on her way up the incline. Her nimble brown legs were galloping under her skirt. Tacit let her go. He wasn't done yet. Carefully he tapped on the glass with his fingernail and a yellow eye appeared with a little start in the darkness.

Halfway up, Camilla turned around and called for him. She thought about the horse—if it got out—if it came after them. Who knew what kind of horse that was?

"Why aren't you coming?"

Tacit came storming up. His eyes sparkled with delight when he reached her.

"Do you know what it was?"

"An animal," said Camilla. "Something ancient that doesn't exist anymore."

"A chicken," said Tacit.

She didn't believe him.

"A chicken? Not that big."

"It was a *hen*. I woke it up."

Camila thought about the tracks in the rooms.

"It was an animal," she insisted. "Something that comes up from the floor at night and walks around in the rooms spreading the dirt. I don't think it was rats."

They made it up to the road, turned around and looked down.

"I don't like that we were down there," said Camilla.

"What harm could it do?"

"We were in the house."

"So what. Now we're here."

"What if someone notices?"

"There wasn't anyone down there. It was totally empty."

"There was a fish and a horse and a hen," said Camilla. "There could have been others."

"Who?"

Tacit knew very well what she meant, and inwardly he knew she was right, but he couldn't admit it. He had to ask.

"Him."

"Aah," said Tacit trying to dismiss it. "A horse and a chicken."

They walked for a while in silence, and he glanced back. But this time the chimney didn't smoke for him. He closed his hand loosely around a grass stem at the road edge.

"Horse or hen?," he asked.

Camilla looked up, and Tacit laughed and pulled the seeds off into his hand.

"What is it?" she asked.

"A horse," he said looking at the ruined seed head.

"How can that be?"

"Look at its tail," he laughed, and showed her.

"How can you be so sure that it was a hen?" she asked seriously, meaning the thing sitting inside the shed.

"I saw it. It jumped down onto the floor."

"Did you open the door?"

"No, are you crazy?"

A bit later he added, "But it was still pretty strange."

CAMILLA AND THE ME-FISH

"Let's go down and swim," he said.
"I'm not allowed."
"It's okay when you're with me."
"That only makes it worse."
He could tell that she wanted to, deep inside. But she was afraid.
"You know that I'm not allowed to," she said quietly, scraping at the gravel with her toe.
"I give you permission."
"I'll get hit if my parents find out."
"They hit you?"
Camilla nodded.
"Last year," he said, and looked at her.
Someone had told her mother.
"Yeah." He tried to coax her. "But this time no one will see us."
"How can you stop them? Or do you have the ability to make people stay home?" She smiled weakly.
"We can just go to another place."
"Where?"
Tacit smiled mysteriously.
"Come and see."
Camilla wavered.
"Come on. You want to." He coaxed her again. "No one will see you."
"Yes," she said. "One."

"I'll close my eyes," he promised.

"It's going to be cold."

"Just put your feet in if you want."

"The river?" she asked.

He shook his head. "No, not really."

"I'm not going in at the beach," she assured him in advance.

"It's not the beach."

"Then where?"

Her curiosity was genuine, and Tacit quickly took advantage of it, pulling her along before she could protest again.

"I'll show you," he said.

They walked through the woods. The dirt on the trail was firm and cool and very dark, and the trees closed gently above them.

"Is it the bog?" guessed Camilla.

"It's a lot farther away. You have never been there before," he said, and kept walking along narrow, twisting trails, deeper and deeper into the woods, until it finally opened out onto a vale with sky above and shining water below. They emerged from the trees and stood on the bank. The water was clear and dark.

Tacit looked at her victoriously.

"What did I tell you?"

"How did you know this was here?"

"I've been here before. I discovered it."

"Did you make it yourself, too?"

Tacit made a broad arm motion out over the water as if he owned it. "Don't you see, it was made for us? We just have to get to the other side."

"Over there?"

"Can't you see the sand—and the sun? And the bottom

isn't steep at all."

The lake was oblong with hills around it. And in the one end where it drained, sand had collected. It felt warm and soft underfoot. Tacit stripped off his clothes and galloped splashing out from the bank until he fell. It was gloriously exhilarating, but just before the water closed over his head he thought about the fish in the stone trough. He lay with his head under water and felt black and quiet as the fish. Did it never move? Or had it been around and around in the trough so many times that it knew it was trapped? It was strange about that fish. He lifted his head and snorted like a horse.

"It's cold," said Camilla.

"Nonsense" snorted Tacit again and wouldn't admit it. She had to come in.

Camilla hesitated.

How should she do this? How was she going to take off her clothes and get in the water? Everything was so different from last year. She fumbled with the buttons at her neck, stalling.

"Come on," prodded Tacit. "It's really nice."

Camilla squirmed. She wanted to. She just didn't know how. He was watching. He lay with his sparkling eyes right down at the water's surface and his mouth below. But he was laughing. She was sure of it. Laughing because she wouldn't take off her clothes.

She went around to the other side of an inlet with some overhanging bushes and commanded him to stay where he was.

"Why?" asked Tacit, splashing in the water as if he were coming after her.

"Otherwise, I won't," she said and she came out into the open so he could see that she hadn't started yet. "Otherwise, I'll go home."

"Fine, I won't," he promised.

As hidden as possible she slipped out of the few clothes she had on and glided down into the water with her braids tied together on top of her head. She stayed down, crawling forward with her arms.

"You look like one of those fog nymphs that dance across the meadow at night with leaves in their hair," said Tacit, swimming over to her. He had never seen her with her hair up before.

Camilla felt around on her braids. To see if anything was there.

"There's no leaves there," she said.

"No, but if there were. That's exactly how they look."

"How do you know?"

She was long and radiant in the shimmering water.

"I've seen them. Sometimes when I go out at night. They ride on calves and lazy workhorses. They stand up on them and dance without falling off."

He came over close to her.

"Oh, that's not true," she said. "You don't have the guts to go out at night."

Camilla's eyes were twinkling. Her bashfulness had left her now that she was under water.And the anxiety that he would look at her was gone.

"You don't think so?" said Tacit. "I've been over at your house a bunch of times too, but you're sleeping."

"Is it true that they have hollow backs?"

"Like a trough," attested Tacit.

"Well, I don't."

"You still look like one."

Tacit reached out his arm through the water and touched her. He stroked her back with his hand.

"You are completely hollow, and your hair is full of leaves

and water plants."

Camilla laughed.

Her skin was smooth. And he could feel her spine when she moved.

"You are such a liar. Don't you think I can tell?"

"A fish could definitely live in your back," he said. "I'm sure of it."

Suddenly she got serious.

"That fish was strange," she said. "It was so black and still. Do you think it was very old?"

"You never know."

He used Granny's tone of voice unconsciously.

"Maybe it lives deep in the ground and just comes up into the trough once in a while," he said.

Camilla looked at him skeptically.

"It could be," he said, trying to erode her doubts, and simultaneously he let his hand follow her ribs around to the front. She stood with her arms on the bottom and scrunched together a little from his touch.

"There's a fish smelling you," he cautioned, softly.

"The you-fish?" she asked smiling awkwardly.

"Yes," he said. "The me-fish. It wants to live in your back."

"It's not *there*," she chirped and moved away. And Tacit had to hold her by putting his whole hand behind her back.

"It's the me-fish," he repeated, pulling her down.

"My hair! My hair!," she yelled and got water in her mouth.

Tacit let her go before her hair went under.

"Are you nuts?" Camilla coughed and sputtered. "If my hair gets wet they'll see it."

"See what?"

"That I was swimming with you."

"Your hair can get wet from swimming by yourself."

Camilla looked at him amused.

"No," she said. "I don't get my hair wet when I swim by myself. Only when I'm with you. You're so wild."

"Besides the fact that it's not even hair," said Tacit.

"Then what is it?"

She took a lock of her bangs and pulled it down so she could see it.

"Mane" he said. "Yellow mane."

It was quiet for a bit and they both suddenly could feel the chill of the water.

"What kind of horse do you think it was?" asked Camilla.

Tacit could hear how her playfulness cooled and how the secretiveness and desolation of the Water Farm took its place in her voice. They stood motionless side by side with only their heads above the water. And they could feel the weak current flowing towards the outlet.

"It was yellow," said Tacit.

That doesn't explain anything, he thought. But he didn't know anyone who had a yellow horse.

"We can visit it again," he said.

"No way," Camilla said quickly.

"Are you afraid?" he teased. "Are you afraid of a completely regular horse?"

"That was no regular horse," she maintained.

"But it looked so nice."

"How do you think it got there?" she wanted to know.

"Out of the pipe like the fish," answered Tacit, flipping unperturbed onto his back, and starting to float.

"I'm not going," said Camilla, not looking at him. "Never ever."

"I didn't know you were a coward," laughed Tacit, turning around and paddling his way next to her.

"Whatever you say," she mumbled, on the verge of getting

irritated.

"Sniff, sniff," he said, putting his mouth against her shoulder.

"If you bite me, I'll hit you."

"You can bite me back," he said into her skin.

"Fish don't bite. In case you didn't know, they don't have teeth."

"Then I'm a horse. Horses love to bite. They have lots of teeth."

He opened his mouth and pressed his teeth into her flesh.

"Once I bit off Ephraim's ear," he said.

Camilla pulled her arm up from the bottom and flopped splashing towards him. Tacit saw her breast come up out of the water and disappear again. She was different than last year.

"That was when I was a dog," he said.

"Right," said Camilla. "You're full of excuses."

"Aren't you allowed to fight like a dog when you *are* a dog?" He carefully snuck his hand underneath her from the side. His fingertips were eyes. And Camilla laughed awkwardly and glided away.

"You have scales on your tail," he called after her.

Laughing, she gave him a look.

"You have no legs, just a tail, and you've returned from the ocean with the salmon. Your hair is black and full of seaweed."

"Are you sure it wasn't me that came up out of that pipe?"

"From the ocean," I said. "Don't interrupt me."

Tacit swam splashing towards her from the front.

"You follow the salmon when they go upstream. You're covered with scales."

He put his hand under her again, but she moved away.

"You have to let your hair down and let it float in the

water," he told her in a hollow voice.

"No way," she chuckled. "It's bad enough as it is."

Tacit swam after her, chasing her out to the deep water, but she swam better than he had figured, and he ended up floating totally still, looking down at the white sandy bottom.

"There are tons of perch," he said.

"You're a perch. I'm freezing."

She started swimming back to shore.

"See for yourself," said Tacit. "They're coming over to us."

"Aren't you scared that they'll bite you," she teased, laughing.

He jumped on her and grabbed her, standing on the bottom while she kicked and twisted.

"Don't scream," he warned her.

Camilla pushed his head down under the water until he let go.

"Are you trying to drown me?" he threatened. He chased her back to the shallow water where she escaped onto the shore in front of him and ran behind the bushes to her clothes.

They dressed in silence.

Afterwards he said, "I know some other lakes besides this one."

"Further in the woods?"

Camilla took her braids and wrung the water out of them.

"Very far into the woods," he assured her. "With pine trees all around."

"And perch?" she asked wryly.

"There's one with mermaids," he said.

"And one with a horse, right?"

"A horse?"

"A yellow one," she said, avoiding him by running away.

I, ÆLGAR—
NO LONGER A PERSON

People say that he was never really a person again after they let him out.

They say that he didn't understand how to get over it and live again.

He.

They mean me.

They claim I am hiding.

But, Ingelin, how can they know anything about that when they have never seen me—or you.

Or have they?

And how can I know what they say when I never talk with anyone? We never had contact with anyone—until yesterday—and he didn't say anything.

Or did he?

Ingelin, living the way we do without dying from it is almost like a science. I am no longer a person and you walk with no horseshoes. Yesterday when we made our way down the narrow grassy edge between the field and the ditch, we lifted the branches carefully so we didn't knock over their stems of grain. We don't want to leave a trail, you know. Not harmful ones anyway. The day's warmth had not yet run out under the low branches, even though the sun had long since disappeared. No one could see us there, but still, we don't trample their grain. That is part of our science.

We had to go to the blacksmith.

The sky above was greenish and clear, and around us the night was just the way we like it—bright enough to light our way and dark enough to hide us. Your hooves had needed to be filed for a long time. We haven't walked enough on their gravel roads, and much too often in soft, silent places. It's not right for ones like us to be seen in broad daylight, and I can tell you, they're afraid of us. They are the ones who won't let us cross over and start living. It's easier to say that old Ælgar isn't a person anymore, and that he's in hiding and he's too strange. And it's easier for old Ælgar to do just that. The two of us live all alone in a land called *sentence served*. That's why we have to go to the blacksmith at night to fix your hooves ourselves when they get too bad off. That's why you've never had shoes. Ingelin, your yellow hide is not meant for the sun. I have made you nocturnal.

But yesterday ....

As a rule we never leave a trace, except for a little hoof filings outside the door. But yesterday—why didn't we turn back when we saw there was a light? Why didn't old Ælgar take you by your bangs and turn you around? No one ever gave us permission to live here. But then, no one ever went through the trouble of coming down here and forbidding it either—not for all these years. And of course they haven't seen us either, when we go wandering around the parish at night, picking green oats for you one straw at a time, or when we laboriously collect the clayey sugar beets that fell off onto the roads in the autumn. It's easier for them just to wait for me to give up and die. That's why they never said we could live here, and that's why they pretend like they don't know.

But why didn't we leave, Ingelin?

A cowering shadow, a long heavy jacket moving silently in front of a small yellow horse. Was it the sound of iron on iron that was so promising? I don't think I had heard that sound since I was a boy. Maybe it was because we have been suppressing every kind of noise in our current existence.

Not heard, not seen, that's the way we live.

And then suddenly, in the middle of the greenish night, the sight of a flame and how the shadows played against the little dirty back window of the smithy. I hadn't expected it, and immediately it changed our errand from something that had to be done, to something that I could watch without being watched. Then the disappointment that I couldn't go close up to window and put my face between the window bars. Against the back wall lay all kinds of rusted iron objects stacked together, keeping me back. And the whole time from inside, the sounds of the work, the sounds of vibrant life casting shadows on the windowpane.

It should have been quiet.

Or there should have been room for my feet by the back wall, so the sounds didn't compel us to go around the house and get a look at the man, the blacksmith. The blacksmith whose rasp and file I would have borrowed, as I have done before, and put back in their places.

This man who is one of the people who says I was never a person again, that I never got over it. He stood in the red-black light while I snuck around his corner to see the pool, this great pool of light that fell on the ground outside the wide-open door.

He stood inside and didn't know I was there. The room enveloped him like a cave. A black woolen darkness from the walls stooped over his forge where the coals lay glowing.

It is much too long since we have allowed ourselves to be illuminated in the darkness, Ingelin. And I didn't dare step into his pool of light. I didn't dare set a foot into the glow of his fire, so as not to scare him. There is so much more than food and clothing one lacks, living like I do. Like we do. You were there with me, Ingelin, even though I forgot about you, so I could cling to the man in there with my people-hungry eyes. I got as close to his pool of light as I dared, standing in the darker dark just outside the glow, taking in the sounds of his banging iron. And I saw his face and his hands, like they were detached, darting back and forth between the forge and anvil with a fire-sparking white piece of iron in a pair of tongs.

From high above, a horseman of the past reached out his broken stirrup down towards his neck, while the sparkling white metal was transformed under his hammer and became redder, seemingly smaller, until it went completely black and was tossed back into the forge.

Or it ended with a sudden hiss in the tub of water.

A shiver penetrated Ælgar, chilling him under his heavy jacket, and he had to pull it more tightly around himself and make the rope tauter at his waist. What a sound!

And Ingelin, that was when you stepped forward curiously into the light from the door.

Your muzzle swayed, outstretched, seeking the strange metallic smells, aware of the man inside. And you didn't notice how all our wretched existence constricted around us in a horrified gasp. You didn't see how terror ignited inside the strong blacksmith who could have crushed your skull with one blow of his hammer.

There we stood, totally visible in the glow of his fear, cloaked in everything that has been thought and said about us in the passage of time, stinking of suppressed life and other people's whispering innuendos.

The blacksmith didn't appear in his door and he didn't put down his large hammer.

He stood paralyzed in the dark hollow staring at us. No one else in the parish has a yellow horse.

After a long pause he asked, "What do you want?"

And the rest of the night and all day today I have been forced to think about what he thought we wanted to do to him. To be someone who has been punished didn't mean to him that the past was settled. It meant a door always open to new misdeeds. Ingelin, how could a person like that think old Ælgar is dangerous.

Behind the blacksmith the coals blackened while he waited, and the building closed in on him, and the silence sang in my head after all the noise. What could we think to tell him so fast? Nothing would be better than the truth, but I wondered if the truth would reconcile him to a couple of night wanderers.

He asked again, and I answered, "Nothing."

Without letting go of his hammer, he pressed on the bellows so the sparks suddenly rose up over the pile of coal. He wasn't going to enjoy our company in darkness, and definitely not with a person without an errand. What I said was not right.

"A coarse file," I said.

My voice hung in my throat like a rusty stake, from lack of use.

"A coarse file," I repeated.

His suspiciousness was obvious from his face. He didn't believe me until I showed him your feet. That kind of thing is upsetting, Ingelin. He wanted to put shoes on you when he saw he was wrong. To make up for it, so you wouldn't hold a grudge. He would have done it even though I couldn't pay him anything. But I was not going to have you shoed with his bad conscience and then go around clattering with his handouts. You are not getting shoed.

But that kind of thing confuses the soul of a blacksmith, and he would have given me the shirt off his back if I had asked him for it.

But I didn't ask.

I didn't think it was worth the trouble to try and explain it to him, how we live like we do, without dying from it. Why should I? Or why the soft sound of a horse's hoof is better than clanking iron when one rides past a sleeping house at night.

Or the taste of frozen sugar beets.

Or of dried pike that has hung flapping in the wind for an entire winter. He wouldn't understand anyway. These things are not a question of whether they taste good or not, but of extending life, without stealing, without stealing anything much, at least.

He asked me where we lived, even though he knew. And I answered truthfully to put him at ease.

"Bring the horse in here," he said.

"That is no horse."

"It's not a horse?"

"That is Ingelin."

"Okay," said the blacksmith still not knowing what I meant. He just lifted your hoof and started using his rasp.

"They say I'm the one who killed her husband."

The blacksmith gave a little start, but tried not to show it. He didn't want to hear any more about it, I could tell. It probably wasn't the best time for confessions.

"But they couldn't prove it," I continued, to put him at ease again. "I was just the one who had to go to jail for it."

The blacksmith didn't say anything. What was there to say?

"Jail," I repeated, thinking about what a spacious word it was, about how much time it could contain, how many years.

"Yeah," said the blacksmith uncomfortably.

Around us the night was full of its own sounds, and here he stood much too close to something he found very disagreeable. It sounded as if he were answering something that I hadn't even asked.

"What is it you are saying 'yeah' to," I asked wondering. "What do you know about jail?"

"Nothing," admitted the blacksmith.

"What do you know about murdering someone?"

He looked at me out of the corner of his eye, but I didn't move.

"Ingelin was a bitch," I continued, to calm him down.

He kept filing nervously, uncomfortable from being under the same roof as a murderer, alone, in the middle of the night.

"She did it," I said.

He didn't believe me. I could tell. He thought I was standing there, absolving myself of blame, putting it on someone else to make myself more virtuous. In any case it was I who took the punishment for it. Whether I did it or not, I was absolved now.

Or was I?

The blacksmith's uncomfortable posture answered me loud and clear. What was once done could never be undone, regardless of how long one sits in jail for it.

"They asked me what I used to do it," I said.

The blacksmith straightened up a little. His eyes searched for the hammer.

"I told them I had used a shovel."

"So where was the body?"

"I told them that I had buried it in the dungheap."

The blacksmith looked at me in horror, repulsed. Yet he was listening with his entire body. It was amazing how closely he was listening.

"'In what dungheap?' they wanted to know."

"In my own, of course, I had said. Where else?"

The blacksmith looked at me with disgust.

"Then why did you say she was the one who did it?" he asked thickly. "What are you saying? Didn't they find him?" The blacksmith forgot himself. His voice was uncomprehending.

"He was in his own dungheap, strangled with a rope."

"So who did it then ...? Her?"

"Ingelin—she was in bed about to give birth when it happened. No one believed it was possible for her to stand upright. No one ever asked her."

"So *was* it her?"

"They had an unhappy marriage."

"But if you knew that already back then...then why ...?"

I had to smile, understanding, excusing this man who only knew what it meant to be a blacksmith, day and night.

"She said that the boy was mine," I told him. "She had just given birth to my son."

You stood with your three legs on the ground, Ingelin, while the blacksmith glared at me in the red light. Your fourth hoof rested comfortably against his leather apron between the patches and the burn holes.

"But she might have lied," I said to his face.

He blinked nervously.

"In any case she married someone else while I was there," I continued.

"In jail," he whispered.

"Yes.," I said. "She didn't wait for me."

"But if you took the punishment on yourself instead of her ... "

"They could never prove anything. But they said that no one else had a reason to kill him except me. I was kind of glad about that."

"Why?"

"I thought that, in that case, it was more likely that it *was* my son."

"Even though she went ahead and married someone else?"

"Maybe it was best that way, when you come down to it."

"Best how?"

"How would it have been for my son with a father who was jailed for murder? He would have hated me."

"But when you didn't do it ...?"

"This way he got both a mother and a father with clean hands."

The blacksmith had to shake his heavy blacksmith head and finish filing.

"And he doesn't hate me," I said.

Then we left without paying except for all the unrest we had unleashed in his soul. His blue-black blacksmith soul. What do you think he made of it, Ingelin? That I was a fool? That back then I wasn't a person either?

GRANNY

Crazy kid ... what's he doing, wrecking her house ....
She held onto the doorframe to help her step over the
threshold into the utility room.

He had said, "Iron."

She stood still, snickering through her nose to herself. As
if that made it okay.

Iron?

That didn't explain anything. Of course it was iron—that
was obvious. But that was no reason to tear it off.

She held on with both hands, wincing. She had been in
such a rush to get out ... it always got worse when she forgot
herself and walked too fast. Now it was both knees.

How could he just go and break off those brackets? Didn't
he understand that it damages the house? He even pulled out
the nails. What did he need them for? Why did he take them
off? What good were they if they weren't attached?

She shook her head. Crazy kid. Then she shuffled over to
her chair by the stove.

It was her house after all ... so far, anyway. It wasn't
in good shape to begin with. He didn't have to make it any
worse with this foolishness. And he never did anything to
help fix it up.

If only he had stopped there.

It was hard to believe he could do something like that.
Tear down the roof over her head? What was going to keep
it all from collapsing one fine day? Those brackets had been
there from the beginning of time attached to the walls. And

then he just goes around and twists them off. She couldn't believe it.

Her hand leaned heavily on the armrest while she lifted her knitting from the straw-stuffed seat where she had thrown it while rushing out to stop him. Then these legs. They were bad again, didn't support her very well. Her fingers arranged the shiny needles in their correct order all by themselves and wrapped the yarn around a finger. Why would he do something like that? How could he?

Her lips kept twitching for a while after her fingers were occupied with the knitting.

He had said, "Iron."

Okay, so what? That's why they were there. He should be able to understand that much.

Plus he had gathered up all of Mikkel's old tools from the eaves and tossed them into a pile on the ground.

Everything was tossed in a pile—it was strange to see it all again. But what was he going to do with it? None of it was any good any more, and it wasn't even his. Aaaah, she was having a lot of trouble with that boy lately. He was always getting into things, and never saying a word about it. She always had to guess.

But she was pretty sure she knew what he planned to do with all that scrap metal he had scrounged together. He probably wouldn't admit that he was going to sell it to that shifty guy from the city who drives through and buys things, but there was no doubt in her mind what he was up to.

"Don't you dare," she had said.

All of Mikkel's chisels and wedges and other hand tools were lying there on the ground between them.

"It's not that," he had said.

"Then what is it? What are you going to do with it?"

He hadn't answered. He had just pressed his lips together.

When she wouldn't budge, after a while he had said, "They're no good for anything anyway."

"Do you want the house to fall down?" she had said.

"The house is standing fine," he had answered.

"Who's to say it's going to keep on standing, the way you're carrying on?" She pointed grimly at the torn-off brackets.

He picked up a big old wedge from the pile.

"Stuff like this isn't good for anything anymore." And he held it up for her to see.

Deep inside she knew he was right. That wedge was no good. It had been used so long that the head on it had broadened like a thick, frayed flower with petals turned down around a short stem. Still, Mikkel had had them with him that day they found him in the woods.

"Put it back," she had said, remaining standing there while he put it all back in the eave again.

And it was to no avail that he got sulky and made a resentful face. She was not going to budge until all the tools were back in place. Some of it looked quite old, things she didn't recognize as Mikkel's. Those had to be back from his father. But if Mikkel kept them, then they were meant to stay there. And no little rascal was going to come and pile it all on the ground and sell it.

"It's not to sell it," he had said.

"Then why is it lying there?" she had asked.

And he had gotten this forebearing, almost sympathetic look around his mouth, which made her feel hopelessly antiquated.

Those were different times back then, when the tools were stuck up under the thatch, and the woods had been a different woods. Much, much bigger and much more dangerous. That was before wolves and wild pigs had been wiped out. What did a boy like him know about the way it was back then? What did he know about what it was like felling trees deep in the woods like that? Nowadays no one lost their life doing it.

It made her think about all the stories that were passed down in Mikkel's family, how the lumberjack tradition was carried on. Stories about how it had been to leave home early in the morning, in the winter, long before it was light, and together with other brawny, bustling fellows make your way between the trees with a lunch sack dangling from a rope around your neck and the big axe and forester's saw over your shoulder.

Mikkel's forester's saw still hung on its nail in the wood shed. And it would keep hanging there as long as she was alive and had any say. But he had been the last.

The first of them arrived long ago with people who wanted land for houses to live in and fields to plant. Mikkel's family had never been much for farm work, and they continued doing what they knew—working in the forest. And she could see before her how son after father had worn down their tools until eventually they were tucked up under the roof eave to stay. How they kept at it until one day or another a tree trunk ended up on top of them, or they chopped themselves in the leg and came crawling home with blood trailing behind them. They were a rugged and taciturn people.

And Mikkel was, too. He never expanded beyond the bit of vegetable garden that originally belonged to the house. The other wives in the area gossiped among themselves that she had a woeful life because of this, and because there was so little left for her when Mikkel was crushed to death by a tree.

He was unable to speak when they found him. His chest was broken and a thin stream of blood ran from his mouth when they laid him in bed.

"What a shame," people said afterwards. "He wasn't even old."

And then Joanna went and got pregnant at the wrong time. They also got a lot of mileage out of that.

"What was she going to do with a baby?" they said. "Why did she keep him? She'll probably have another one before long."

They were wrong.

Joanna never came back. The city kept her, and she heard from somewhere that Joanna got married.

"Of course she never had to tell the man that she had a child already," people said maliciously. Talk like that was cheap and convenient.

Granny never answered statements like that. And she never told anyone why she had kept the child, after first vowing that Joanna had to take the child with her. She never forgot that day when Joanna had stood in the doorway, with her fat belly and her cardboard suitcase, how restless and strange she was while waiting for the baby to be born, as if it were something she just had to get over with.

And how she had cried and carried on when Granny insisted that she had to take care of the child herself.

It was only when the boy was lying there on the bed without a sound that she knew what kind of child it was. None of her own children had been as quiet and patient when they were little. It was Mikkel's temperament. His quiet, laconic way of being had come through. But evidently mixed together, she noticed later, with quite a bit of other influences.

A new little Mikkel.

Granny had kept him without caring what the other women said and thought.

"At her age," they said.

She thought about how empty she would have felt without him.

"You should have beat some sense into him while you still could," they said later.

"Now you're stuck. You should have given him a few whacks. All that talk does nothing."

"What are you going to do with a kid?"

"You could have just said no. Why did you have to go ahead and take him? Now you can see for yourself what you get for doing things like that."

Granny smiled inwardly. They didn't understand.

But he was always up to something. She was continually running after him so he didn't get into trouble too deep. And at the moment he was out of control. There was a restlessness about him lately, and what about when he finished school? What then? He wasn't going to go out and work on a farm like other young people. That's what he said, anyway.

"Well, then what?" she had asked.

He hadn't answered.

She jumped in her chair, startled by a thud. Was he up in the attic? She sat listening. Now he was over her head.

"What are you doing?" she asked from below.

"Nothing," he answered, dragging something heavy across the thin boards.

"Then get down here," she said.

"Okay," he said from up there. But he didn't come down.

He kept bumping around with things. But what could he use that was up in the attic? Only worn out and broken things, which had been accumulating for many years, were up there. What could he do with them?

With difficulty she eased her way out of her chair by the stove and placed herself in the doorway to the living room with her yarn squeezed under her arm and her knitting needles sticking out between her fingers. In the sun's rays, dust floated down golden and peaceful. Dirt and sawdust lay thick on the tablecloth.

"You're making a mess!" she yelled, thrusting forward her fat bottom lip in exasperation.

It got quiet up there for a moment.

"Are you almost done?"

She observed uneasily the whitewashed ceiling boards giving dangerously beneath his movements back and forth. Wooly clumps of dust fell from the edges. It looked unsafe.

"I'll come down and sweep," he promised from above.

She snickered dismissively. She knew very well what became of promises like that when it came down to it. Pretty soon he would put a leg through the ceiling, or come crashing down, him and all that junk, and then what? Those punky boards can't hold much anymore, and who is going to build her a new attic when he destroys the old one? But he didn't think about things like that.

And what about him when he gets seriously hurt?

Displeased, she quietly sat back down. He won't ever listen to her, but he will gladly take apart every inch of the house.

It made her think of Mikkel, the time they carried him in. She had sat next to the bed and seen the blood seeping out of his mouth. She had seen his color change, and there was nothing she could do.

Something heavy crashed to the ground out by the gable end, shaking the house.

The sound came from out by the hatch.

In the kitchen she started running while she was still sitting in her chair, yarn wrapped around her index finger. Her legs moved, her heart jumped, leading her out the door, through the utility room to the sound of the fall. The ultimate, final fall that spread through the floor to her chair and rose up through the chair to her body. The horrible certainty,— for she knew it was coming, had already known it for a long time. And she had said it—said it to him—that he had to be careful. But he never listened.

The yarn rolled indecisively trailing her swollen, uncooperative slippered feet. It unraveled, didn't want to follow her out. Just the knitting.

"Well good Lord, boy .... "

But he wasn't laying on the ground like she had expected. He wasn't stretched out with blood trickling from his mouth. A thin stream that wouldn't stop.

There was a crate with heavy pieces of metal.

She stared at it. That bump ....

His grinning face appeared in perfect condition through the open hatch.

"What's the problem?"

"Problem?" She had to hold on tight to the doorjamb with one hand to keep from falling. It wasn't him. It wasn't his fault. Not this time either.

"Did you think it was me?"

His voice smiled, reconciling himself to her folly.

"I won't fall, I told you."

And inside Granny there was anger, because he had frightened her. And she flung her words at his grinning face because he just didn't understand.

"But I didn't fall down," he said in his defense.

"What do you want with all that junk?"

The boards in the crate had burst when it hit the ground, and the rusty nails stuck out into the air.

"What are you bringing it down for?"

His face got a secretive look.

"Nothing," he said.

"Why don't you ever do anything to help?"

Suddenly he stiffened up in the hatch at the sight of blood dripping from her hand with the knitting.

"Granny, you're bleeding ... "

The horror in his voice made her look down. And only

now she noticed the knitting that she hadn't managed to put down. It hung from her hand.

A knitting needle had poked through the fat part of her middle finger and stuck there while the rest of the sock slipped to the floor.

Tacit jumped down beside her in a flash.

"But Granny ...."

She took hold with the other hand and pulled out the needle.

"You pulled it out?" he asked in disbelief.

"Of course I did."

He stared amazed at the place where it had been. Blood seeped out of both sides of her finger.

"So you just pulled it out?" he asked again and couldn't get over her lack of emotion.

"Well, I can't go around with it sticking out like that, can I." she hissed and left to rinse her hand at the pump.

"But didn't it hurt?"

She mumbled irately, rinsing the needle too, while he stood and watched. Then he picked up her knitting off the ground and stood there while she put the stitches back on the needle.

"Look at that," she said, showing him the blood on the yarn. "That looks terrible. You see what happens? What do you expect from all this nonsense?"

She turned away from him and walked into the house shutting the door behind her. Which she usually never did.

From inside she could hear him wandering indecisively around for a little while. Then suddenly he went and lit the stove. And he made it pretty hot, she thought, opening all the vents, emptying the peat box into it and getting more. The chimney roared vehemently and warmth began to spread inside the little house.

She sighed resignedly and walked out to feel the cleanout cover with her other hand's tentative fingers.

"Boy, you're crazy."

"What's wrong?"

"You're going to burn down my house with those shenanigans."

"It *has* to be hot," he said, noticing a bit of peat dust he had spilled on the stove top. It flared up for a brief moment into small bluish flames, then shrunk down leaving behind the smell of burnt peat.

He lifted the middle ring on the stove to check on his fire, and a long thin curl of flame flickered up at him.

Billows of smoke flowed in waves over the woods behind their garden, and Granny apprehensively watched the weak spots in the stovetop that were already starting to glow red.

You couldn't light a stove like that.

Yet he still went out for more. Through the window she saw him heading for the peat shed, and almost simultaneously towards the girl out by the road.

She went into the living room again and shut the door.

He didn't come back in. The house got quiet. And much much later she went over and took off the rings.

There were lots pieces of iron lying in the coals, and out on the stone steps Mikkel's hammer and tongs were ready.

She stood there looking, thinking for a long while.

A blacksmith?

Someone who made stakes and chisels ... and shoes people's workhorses?

She was still sitting in the living room when he finally returned.

YELLOW INGELIN

The horse's window was empty and black.
He stood there anyway, for a long time, unmoving,
staring at it, waiting for something to show itself from behind
the dirty glass: the long, yellow face with the easy-going
eyes. He knew nothing was going to happen. It wasn't going
to look at him today. Nothing was going to appear.

It was dead.

To Tacit the black window was like a deserted place inside
himself—a loss. He had apples with him, too, and bread
crusts—his pockets were bulging.

Ordinary horses didn't live in farmhand's quarters, he
knew that much. Still he was sure that it *had* been there that
day. Not a huge horse, but a horse, a yellow one.

But what if it weren't totally dead? What if it were lying in
there and could hear him but couldn't get up? Maybe it was
just about to die of hunger because no one came to feed it.

And his pockets were full.

But maybe it was already too late.

As quietly as possible he opened the hasp and looked in
through the door crack. He couldn't see anything. He opened
wider. Light from the window shone into the little room with
a soft certainty, fractioning itself invitingly over the thick
layer of straw covering the entire floor.

It wasn't there.

Not in the room behind it either. Shyly, Tacit let his eyes
wander through the half-open door to the next room. That

must be where *he* lived—the man. A crude bed stood against one wall. It was a big solid crate of thick boards with straw inside. A chair with a leg broken in half was supported by a wooden block.

He retracted his gaze. Not that he was afraid. But he didn't really like being in there. What would he say if the man suddenly arrived. He didn't even know what he looked like. Just the horse.

He would have liked to have given it the apples and maybe patted it. But maybe it would come back. He took the apples and bread crusts and laid them in the windowsill where it could get them.

Then he went out and looked at the window from the outside. You couldn't tell that there was anything lying there. That was good.

He walked over to the water and peered down into the trough.

The fish?

There was no fish.

Not one single black shadow that could have been the fish, only the old leaves on the bottom, brown and rotting.

He leaned over to check more closely, staring through his own distorted reflection.

Nothing.

He felt the crack in the trough with his hand. Did it get out that way with the flowing water? Did it discover that the edge of the trough, this big old hollowed-out stone that let the water from inside the earth run through it, was broken?

He stood there a long while. Until above the water's melodic splashing he heard other sounds, a soft thumping of uneven bone-like steps that turned in through the gate to the farmyard.

That's it, he thought.

Without horseshoes.

A horse that walked like a cow, as if it lived in a place where there were no blacksmiths. Or where a horse didn't need shoes. He turned around and saw it.

"Yellow," he said.

A blanket hung down its one side dragging on the ground. And the reins were broken. The rope dangled down in two loose ends from its muzzle. It turned itself around uneasily when it heard him.

That was when he realized that it was alone, that the man wasn't there. Something had happened someplace, he didn't know where, and the horse had returned without its rider.

He walked carefully over towards it, but the yellow horse didn't want him to touch it. It swung its head nervously and jumped sideways when he grabbed its mane.

"But you can't just walk around with that thing trailing behind you," he said gently, patting it reassuringly while he reached for the blanket that hung off its side. It had been torn by being walked on.

And it was soaking wet.

"Yellow horse, where have you been? Tell me, where have you been?"

He spoke calmly while he loosened the blanket, and the horse anxiously moved its head from side to side. It had been in the water somewhere. It was still wet down its sides, and Tacit almost didn't dare think about where the man was now and what had happened to him. His fingers feverishly took up the broken reins and tied the stiff, wet ends together. They weren't just dipped in the water, whey were waterlogged. And the whole time he murmured to keep the horse calm. He had to hurry, had to ride back and find the trail if he could. And not think, don't try to imagine what happened, because that made his knees go weak.

Just get up on the horse.

The yellow horse wanted nothing to do with him. It twisted and turned—good Lord would you stand still, horse, you're wasting time—stand still, dammit, you're stepping on me.

He tried again.

The yellow horse just got even wilder, and he realized that he would have to be content with just leading it by the halter. He led it out through the gate, there was only one route to choose. The hoofprints showed clearly from which way it had come, but the horse was stubborn and resisted. It didn't want to go back to whatever had frightened it.

Could it be he was dead? Is that what it knew? It must have sensed that before it left him.

Lying on the road with a broken neck?

There was no one on the road.

The horse was wet, and the blanket was wet.

Then in the water?

What water?

He tried to empty his thoughts and just follow the trail, but the possibilities would not let him be. One horrible vision followed another, until he started to sweat.

The trail stopped.

Without his noticing, the ravine had widened to a broader swampy terrain. He stood still and shouted as loud as he could.

From someplace out there he heard some kind of sound.

The yellow horse lifted its head, wanting to run away. Tacit had to force it. "But it's him," he murmured softly, "It's the man, your man, what are you running away for?" He pulled the horse with him onto the soft ground between tall reeds and alder trees on stilted roots. There were pools of water that he had to avoid. Someplace out there was the stream, the river, and in it the water from the farm. The water. The most zealous water around.

People had once dug peat out here in the past. The big rectangular pits were still here, filled with black water and with narrow walls a yard wide between them. The horse's hide twitched nervously and it averted its eyes. This was no place for a horse, but Tacit didn't let go. His one hand was almost dead from pulling, but he had to have the horse as an alibi, for himself, too. Why else would he come to this place?

The old man was lying floating in a peat pit with his hands clutching the grass on the edge. Tacit's legs sunk down deep into the mud because he didn't look where he was going, and he had to brace himself with the horse to pull himself out. The old man's face was white against the black water, and his long beard floated on the surface.

They looked at one another. No one asked anything. The old man's eyes expressed no relief at the sight of him. But he did answer, thought Tacit. Mostly he looked at the horse, and with a strangely resigned sigh, as if things had not gone as he had planned.

He must have been hanging there for a long while. Only his eyes were moving.

How long had the yellow horse been swimming around next to him before it got out?

A wide gash in the rim showed where the horse and rider had fallen in—or maybe it was there it had climbed out. It was hard to tell. The boy felt a pitiful pang in his chest at the thought of the horse clawing and clawing with its hoofs without meeting firm ground. The dirt had collapsed into the water in big chunks, dissolving to mud. The entire breach was gone, dissolved or fallen to the bottom. He was sure it was deep.

And next to it the old man was hanging onto clumps of grass.

Why hadn't he grabbed the horse and let it help him out? Without letting go of the halter Tacit bent down and took hold of the collar of the heavy long coat.

The old man opened his mouth in the center of the floating beard and gave out a startling roar that made Tacit fall to his knees. The water rushed into his open mouth and the sound disappeared in a gurgling cough. He stopped pulling.

"Goddammit, kid ... "

"Yes?"

Tacit looked at him questioning. A hat floated, rocking on the water a little further down. The old man's voice was hoarse and strained.

"It's-s the horse," he stuttered. "It sm-mashed my one knee."

"I have to pull," said Tacit.

"It kicked me, don't you hear?"

"It's the only way I can get you out."

The old man cursed his painful leg and the horse that had broken it and finished by spilling his anger out onto Tacit who could just keep his hands to himself.

Tacit stared at him anxiously. What did he mean by that? Didn't he want to be helped? Was he trying to drown himself? Then why was he holding on to the grass for so long?

The horrible thought that he could be left standing there, seeing the old man let go and floating away from the edge gave him the strength of desperation. He was not going to accept that the old man was going to let himself die. He had to do something.

To see the icy black water flow through his beard, into his mouth again—and stay there? No one would ever know what happened.

Tacit grabbed the collar harder and pulled again.

The old man yelled, trying to keep his bad leg clear of the edge by pushing against it with the other one, but the ground he touched kept eroding into the watery pit. Tacit pulled wildly.

But, in the soaked longcoat, the old man's body was heavily weighed down, and the muddy water resisted.

The man's hands clenched the grass in pain while a torrent of curses flowed from his mouth.

Tacit didn't let it get to him. The horse planted its hooves in the peaty ground and leaned away, and Tacit felt his shoulder bones almost dislocating. He felt like he was going to be pulled apart. The yellow horse thought it was going to be thrown into the water, he thought. That's why.

The old man's fingers were still gripping the tufts of grass and Tacit stammered to him to let go. Yelled to him to let go of the grass. But the man's fingers did not straighten.

"You're working against me," he yelled.

His hands didn't open. Maybe he didn't hear him. Maybe he didn't want to. His cursing rose in volume and then fell to a mumble, and the boy's outstretched arms were almost not arms anymore, but a rope between too heavy a burden and a petrified horse. Then the rim gave way, the grass fell in with roots and everything. The horse stepped backwards and the water reluctantly relinquished its prey.

He lay on the ground as if he were dead, his hands still gripping two big clumps with tough yellow stems. Tacit stood for a while looking at him uncertainly. Then he tied off the horse.

Was the man dead? Was it all for nothing? Or was it because he was angry over not being allowed to drown in peace? That could be. The old sunken face was pale, eyes closed and there was brown mud in his beard.

But he was breathing.

Tacit stood for a while waiting for him to say something. To tell him what to do next. How to do the next thing. He was a man and Tacit was only a boy who did what he was told. At any rate now that the old man was pulled out. He didn't think it was up to him to decide anymore.

But the man didn't move.

Tacit bent down doubtfully over him and saw that he was sleeping. He was cold as ice from being in the water for so long, and Tacit realized that he wasn't done being in charge.

"You can't sleep," he said, shaking the old man's shoulder.

A suppressed shudder is all that he got in response. The man was not going to wake up willingly.

"You have to go home," said Tacit.

"Leave me alone. Go away."

"But you can't lay here. You're wet."

Tacit felt powerless over the man's unmanageable body and was about to cry. He couldn't carry him. He couldn't even lift him up onto the horse or get him across the boggy ground to the road. If only he had a sled, a wagon plank or an old door that he could tie to the horse. But he didn't have anything. And the horse didn't have a harness. He was going to have to make the old man stay awake. He pulled on his shoulder again.

"You have to wake up now," Tacit said. "You have to go home."

"I would rather die." the old man said.

"You can sit on the horse," Tacit suggested.

"It crushed my knee."

"But you can still sit on it."

"The devil I can. I'm done for."

He was dismissive and unfriendly, but Tacit was not giving up yet.

"You'll freeze lying here in those wet clothes."

"Freeze," the old man yelled up in Tacit's face. "It crushed my knee, do you hear? It almost killed me and then you come here bothering me. Leave me alone, you hear? You could have left me out there and then it would have all been over."

"But ... "

"Let me die, goddammit."

"What about your horse?"

"Ingelin—she should be drowned, that bitch -"

"It came and got me," said Tacit.

"Ingelin ... "

The old man's voice trailed off, and the horse lowered its head and sniffed the old man's face cautiously. The smell of peatwater scared it, but it knew his voice.

"Do you want her to die of starvation so you can be allowed to lie here?" asked Tacit and made a stern face.

"We're both going to anyway," the old man hissed.

"Why?"

"I can't walk on that leg."

"I can help you get home."

"And then what? Is it better to rot in a bed? You should have just left me out there. Drowning is faster than starving."

"I can bring you food," said Tacit.

"Liar. No one gives me anything."

"Yes," said Tacit. "I will."

"Not when you find out who I am."

"I know who you are. I left bread and apples for the horse on the window sill."

The man leaned up on one elbow.

"You're lying. You're just saying that. No one has ever given me bread or apples."

"Then come home and see," said Tacit.

"Home where?" The old man bored his angry gaze into Tacit.

The boy hesitated a second.

"The Water Farm," he said.

"Who is your father?"

"I don't have one."

"Then your mother?"

"I live with my granny. I always have."

"In what house?"

"The little one by the woods."

"I'll burn it down over your heads if you're lying to me."

"Fine."

"What are you saying fine to?"

"I'm not lying. I'll tell Granny to kill a chicken."

The old man's eyes followed him in disbelief.

"A chicken?"

"She'll make soup out of it," said Tacit.

The man sat up without even realizing it, and a warm gladness filled the boy. He had won.

"I can't bend my leg," said the man.

"We can tie on some sticks," said Tacit, "to keep it straight."

He started cutting the reins for rope. And as carefully as possible he tied two sticks to the bad leg.

"There," he said, and bent down the horse's head, so the old man could take hold of the halter. Then he put his shoulder underneath him and helped lift.

When the old man was lying on his belly over the horse, he passed out, and no matter how Tacit pushed or pulled it was no use. He would just have to stay like that.

Very carefully he led the horse back to the road and up through the ravine to the farm. It wasn't until they made it in to the farmyard that the old man started to moan.

Water was still dripping from him, and Tacit was hoping that he wouldn't come to until he had gotten him all the way into his room. But he wasn't sure how to do it. The man was feeble from having laid in the peat pit for so long and the cold made him shiver so his teeth were chattering.

The yellow horse stopped outside the door on its own.

"Open up," stammered the old man. His beard covered his eyes as he hung there head down. Still he knew where he was.

Tacit opened the door. And the yellow horse lifted its hooves over the threshold one at a time, while Tacit guided it in so the bad leg didn't get pressed or scraped too much.

"Lift me down," demanded the battered rider between his bluish lips. And inch by inch Tacit lowered him to the thick layer of straw covering the floor. Meanwhile it was as if the yellow horse understood that it shouldn't move.

Still the pain was so great that the man lost consciousness again when he made it to the ground and lied down.

Tacit pushed the horse aside and started loosening the rope that held the long waterlogged coat around the man's waist. He carried it out and dropped it with a splash onto the cobblestones in the farmyard. And to his amazement he discovered that this unwieldy garment was the old man's only clothing aside from his pants. He wasn't sure what he was expecting, but it wasn't that.

"Them too," mumbled the supine figure almost inaudibly, as he fumbled ineffectively with his waistband with stiff, weakened fingers.

Tacit pulled and slipped them down around the broken knee, barely touching it at all, he thought, but the old man clenched his fists down into the straw and yelled. Then Tacit threw them out next to the coat.

The old man lay there, eyes closed, and Tacit stood for a while, not knowing what else to do. The spindly old body lay stretched out in the straw and seemed as helpless as he knew it was, so aged and fragile. He wondered if it would be a good idea to rub his skin with some straw. Strange that the poor skinny guy could be so heavy.

"What are you staring at?" sneered the old man without opening his eyes.

"Your knee," mumbled Tacit, carefully starting to wipe the mud off with clumps of straw. The knee was swollen and dark compared to the rest of his body.

"I'm cold," said the man shivering. "Bring me the other one."

"The other what?"

"On the bed, you idiot."

Tacit came back with another coat, heavy and long like the other, laid it over him and placed straw on top.

"Wouldn't you rather get into bed?" he asked just to be sure.

"No," said the man.

"Well, what about the horse?"

"Leave me alone."

"What if it lays on top of you?"

"Shut up and get out."

The horse was over at the window quietly chewing the remains of an apple.

"What are you feeding her?" screamed the old man suddenly, leaning up on an elbow.

"The apples," said Tacit.

The old man glared at him. "I thought you were lying."

Tacit took half of the food and laid it down next to the invalid, but he didn't eat it. He took a piece of bread in his hand. The chill was still rumbling through him in waves of shivers, and Tacit piled on as much straw as he could. Then he quietly sat himself with his back against the wall, waiting.

It took a long time before the warmth returned to him, but with all the more force when it finally did come. The man on the floor got restless under his little pile, his cheeks blushed and his eyes shone without seeing.

It's fever, thought Tacit. And he knew he would have to stay for quite a while yet.

Afterwards he would to go home to Granny and tell her about the chicken. And with three kind of dumplings, he decided.

THE FEMALE CENTAUR

When Tacit was done with school he went to the smithy and asked to become an apprentice.

"What for?" asked the blacksmith, lowering his arm with the hammer, looking at him suspiciously.

"I don't like farmwork," said Tacit.

The blacksmith snickered dismissively and Tacit felt like he should say more, explain himself. Everyone around here does farmwork—all except for the blacksmith. He should be able to see that.

"It's too hard," he said.

"You mean you don't feel like working hard?" asked the blacksmith.

"I don't like cows," said Tacit. "What's the point of spreading manure or hoeing sugar beets?"

"If you think you're going to convince me by telling me that, you're wrong, " said the blacksmith."I can't use lazy people."

"I'm not lazy," said Tacit.

"Oh, no?"

The blacksmith lifted an eyebrow and laid the iron back on the forge.

"I just don't want to be a farmhand like all the others," explained Tacit. "I want to make things."

"Make things? That's hard, too."

"Only if you don't want to."

Tacit was not going to let himself be dissuaded by the

blacksmith's rebuffs. The blacksmith grabbed the iron bar over his head and pumped air through the coals, so small blue flames danced around the black iron.

"Okay—and you think you do."

"Yes," said Tacit without wavering.

"You also need ability," continued the blacksmith.

"I know," said Tacit, looking at the blacksmith's powerful forearm.

"And strength …."

"That'll come with time," replied Tacit.

The blacksmith measured him up mockingly without letting go of the bellows.

"You weren't born with arms like that, were you?" continued the boy, standing by the door.

"You don't insult honorable farmwork," said the blacksmith as if he hadn't heard him.

The boy at the door went silent, waiting.

"You don't!" roared the blacksmith turning his head.

"Then why are you a blacksmith?" asked Tacit.

The man leered at him.

"Well, someone's got to shoe their horses," he admitted.

"Would you rather be spreading manure?" asked Tacit.

"You heard me, didn't you?" yelled the blacksmith. "Go on home."

Tacit didn't move.

"What about when you get old?" he asked, knowing that the blacksmith didn't have any sons.

"What business is that of yours? I'll get apprentices myself when I need them. Who said I need anyone now?"

"No one," admitted Tacit.

"Well, then what are you hanging around for? Go along home, I said."

"But I'm the one who needs it," said Tacit.

A vein began to bulge on the blacksmith's forehead.

"I need to become an apprentice now," continued Tacit quickly. "When you are so old that you need someone to help you it will be too late."

For a second he thought that the blacksmith was going to take a swipe at him. But the man's large fist rammed the tongs down between the coals and picked up a white glowing piece of iron instead. The blacksmith's blows filled the room to its bursting point while Tacit stood with a blessed paralyzation in his body, following how the white iron changed color and shape with handling, how it bent around the horn of the anvil.

For a long time all that existed in the world was the sound.

"You can come on trial basis for a month," said the blacksmith suddenly, slinging the iron into the forge again.

It sounded like a threat, and Tacit didn't dare say a word before he was sure of what he had heard.

"But if you think it's easier to shoe their horses than to tend their cows, you're wrong," said the other inhospitably. "It takes hard work."

Tacit ignited inwardly.

Granny had said that he could just as well forget about it, that the blacksmith would never take him, that he could just as well find a place on a farm right away and give up running around, making himself look foolish.

Granny had said —

"Now get out of here," yelled the blacksmith. "And remember it's only on a trial basis."

Tacit tore himself away from the doorway and sped home. He did not doubt for one second that he would pass the trial period and become a real apprentice. He believed in his future, and he felt waves of happiness all through him whenever he thought about when the blacksmith said "their horses" and "their cows." It was the farmers. The blacksmith and Tacit were separate from them.

Their horses.

And *their* cows.

The blacksmith himself didn't notice anything when he said it, but Tacit noticed immediately and knew that everything had already been decided.

Granny wasn't so sure.

"Don't blow your horn before it's time," she said.

"I'm not," ensured Tacit. "It's just that you're too old to realize it."

"I'm not too old to hear and see. That blacksmith has never had an apprentice, even though lots of boys wanted to."

"They weren't good enough."

"How do you know?"

"Farmer boys with dirt in their souls," mumbled Tacit.

Granny smirked.

"Dirt matters more than anything," she said angrily. "No one knows that better than me."

"But not for a blacksmith. When you own land, your movements get slow and cumbersome.And that's no good."

"But you think you're good?"

Tacit laughed.

And when the trial period passed without incident and no one said anything about him stopping, she had to admit he was right. The blacksmith hadn't said anything about a month being up, and Tacit wasn't about to remind him. Time passed while they worked side by side. But people wondered.

The blacksmith was known as a man of few words and a troubled mind. But since Tacit wasn't much for conversation either, the atmosphere in the smithy was fine, until the day that the blacksmith happened to find a little female figure with four arms and a horse's body that lay on the filing bench where Tacit had his work area. The blacksmith picked it up before he really saw what it was.

"What the hell—"

He dropped the figurine as if it been burning hot, then stared menacingly at it as if he had expected it to start moving, and roared for Tacit.

"What the devil is this piece of garbage?"

Tacit lowered his hammer and came over.

"Oh, that thing … "

To the blacksmith's amazement, Tacit didn't seem particularly guilt-ridden, not more than if he had dropped a piece of his lunch on his tools. And not at all as if he had been caught red-handed.

"What is that supposed to be?"

Tacit could hear that the blacksmith was quite agitated, and not only agitated but also shocked. He hadn't expected that. From the farmers maybe, if they had the misfortune of seeing the figurine, but not the blacksmith. He quietly took the small object up in his hand and explained that it wasn't anything special, not yet.

"It's not? Do you think that obscenity is nothing special?"

"Obscenity?"

Tacit looked amazed at the figurine and up at the blacksmith. "This isn't obscene. It's just a figure."

But the blacksmith knew very well what he was looking at. He sneered, "If that's not obscenity, to display naked women, and on top of that with four arms..."

"And you do that during work hours?"

The blacksmith's tone of voice was not promising.

"No. After work."

Tacit still didn't appear regretful in the least and the blacksmith roared that he should be ashamed of himself.

"But this isn't dangerous or anything," protested Tacit.

The blacksmith's eyes looked crazed.

"Obscenity!" he sneered between his clenched teeth. "And with a horse."

"It's a centaur," Tacit informed him and stood the figurine up on the filing bench.

The blacksmith leered at it.

"A what do you call it?"

"A female centaur."

"Now watch your mouth.Don't think you can trick me into anything. Don't come here and tell me you have ever seen a thing like that in real life."

"Only in pictures," admitted Tacit.

"You lie," said the blacksmith."That doesn't exist."

There was more hope that actual certain knowledge in his voice and Tacit repeated that he had seen pictures of several of them.

"Where?"

The blacksmith stared intently and disbelieving from under his bushy eyebrows. His eyes narrowed.

"With Teacher Melin."

"Are you claiming that Teacher Melin shows obscene pictures to his children—at the school?"

"No," said Tacit, taking a deep breath.

"Then don't say things like that."

"It's not obscene," maintained Tacit. "It's a figurine, and it's in some books that Teacher Melin has at his house."

"That disgusting city slicker—he should be ashamed of himself. You're not old enough to be exposed to things like that."

Tacit stood there not knowing what to say. Teacher Melin never said the slightest thing about anything being wrong with those pictures—quite the contrary.

"And then completely naked ... " sneered the blacksmith,

"and with hair ... horse's legs ... how could he, Melin, why would he show you something like that?"

"Because I went into the church one day, and he came in afterwards."

"What does that have to do with it?"

The blacksmith instinctively pulled his head down towards his shoulders, prepared for anything.

"To see what I should do."

"And what did you have to do?"

"Look at the figurines."

"In the church?"

"Yes."

"There's no 'figurines' in the church."

"Yes, there are," said Tacit.

The blacksmith was getting hot under the collar.

"Are you going to tell me that you have seen one of these around in the church?" he roared.

"Well, no, not that one, but ones like these," said Tacit, pulling out the drawer under his workbench, fishing out a couple of entwined, twisted, cat-like creatures.

"You're lying!" screamed the blacksmith, staring down his apprentice with wide horrified eyes. "This is pure blasphemy!"

"Then go see for yourself," said Tacit quietly. "They're on the baptismal font."

"Not ones like this," mumbled the other.

"Go look for yourself. You just never noticed them before. That's why."

"Well you could have made something from the altarpiece instead. You don't always have to pick the worst thing."

Tacit rummaged around in his drawer silently and pulled out a couple of long-bearded men with apostle capes and placed them down next to the other things.

The blacksmith stared at him speechless.

"The saints?"

"Yes," said Tacit.

"And they lie in the drawer with naked women with four arms and horses' legs?"

Tacit shrugged his shoulders. He didn't see that it mattered. It was quiet for a while.

"What are you going to do with all that?" the blacksmith wanted to know.

"Nothing. I just wanted to try and copy them."

"But what are you going to use them for?"

"Nothing."

The blacksmith waved his hands ineffectually in the air as if he were bothered by flies. He couldn't understand why anyone would undertake so much work for no reason. Because it was a great deal of work. That much he could see.

He ventured to wrap a hand around one of the saints.

"Who told you how to make a casting?"

"Nobody," said Tacit.

The blacksmith looked at him cautioningly.

"Then where did you learn how?"

"I read about it."

"And the metal?"

The blacksmith had noticed long before that it didn't come from his smithy.

"It's Granny's old hanging lamp and things like that— from the attic at home."

"She let you?"

Tacit just smiled and the blacksmith shook his stout head. Unfathomable what a lad like that could get into.

"Maybe I'll sell them some day," said Tacit a bit later.

The blacksmith's head stopped with a jerk and his eyes were dubious.

"Sell? Is there someone who would buy things like that?"

"You never know."

"And pay money?"

Tacit smiled secretively, thinking about the little gray man with the thin glasses that he had gone to see the last time he was in town with Granny. This gentle silver-gray individual who had led him down a long corridor, where all kinds of strange objects were stacked, to a room with a window out towards the back.

Tacit had first been in the store trying to sell two of his prophet-like apostles, but the man immediately rolled them up in the towel again, looking around anxiously.

"Not here," he had said.

And with no further explanation he had pulled Tacit along with him to the back room, where there were just as many odd objects crammed together as in the corridor and the store itself. But back here there was a fine layer of fluffy gray dust on everything. Even the light felt dusty.

The little man had meticulously and myopically examined the saints for a long time before he turned around and asked Tacit if he had any more.

"Not with me," said Tacit.

"But you can get them?"

"It depends ... " said Tacit, thinking about how long it took to make them.

The little gray man sized him up out of the corner of his eye and didn't say anything right away.

Eventually he said in a strange hesitant manner, "Well, this kind of thing is not without its dangers."

"What's dangerous about it?" asked Tacit.

"Well, I'm sure you know what I mean," the man responded.

Tacit stared uncomprehendingly at him for so long

that the man had to clear his throat and attempt a kind of explanation, that when one deals in so many different kinds of things it's not always that easy to keep track of where they come from.

"Come from?" repeated Tacit.

"These pieces are all so old," the man said smiling, indicating with a wave of his hand what was stacked together along the walls.

"Not these," said Tacit quickly, referring to the figurines.

"They're not? Where did you get them?" The man sounded politely interested.

"Well, I make them myself," Tacit blurted out, thinking that the man ought to have known that much.

"Yes, of course," the little man rushed to say, "Of course you make them yourself." Then he lowered his voice. "But still you can tell *me* where they're from," he whispered, confidentially taking hold of Tacit's arm.

"But it's true," assured Tacit, ill at ease. What did that second-hand dealer actually think?

"Sure, sure, of course it is … but tell me anyway … it makes a difference in the price."

The man's blue childlike eyes examined again the figurines he held in his hands.

Then he asked, "How many are left?"

"None," said Tacit.

"But you just said …." The little man seemed disappointed.

"I can make as many as you want. I just need time to do it," explained Tacit. "But I don't have any more right now."

The gentle little man's face grew dark with anger.

"If you don't think I can tell the difference between fakes and genuine cast work, then you are mistaken young man!" he sputtered lividly. "I know the difference when I see it, and you can just as well go tell it to whoever you got them from."

"Aren't they good enough?" asked Tacit cautiously. "Is there something wrong with them?"

"Good enough? They're too good. That's what I'm talking about. They're too exquisite for you to have made them. You broke them off someplace."

The dealer's thin voice cracked with outrage while he shook the one apostle threateningly in his clenched hand. He was certain they were stolen, but that wasn't what incensed him. Tacit realized that what made him angry was the fact that he, Tacit, kept insisting that he made them himself.

"There is no way that you could make one of these," continued the second-hand dealer.

"Yes, I can," responded Tacit. "As many as you want. I'm a blacksmith."

The man before him snickered.

"The devil you are. Blacksmith. Would you have me believe that blacksmiths can make sculptures like these— and out here in the country? I won't have anything to do with this until you tell me the truth."

"And what if I actually am telling the truth?"

"We can talk about that when you prove it."

Tacit smiled.

"How about we do a little test?" he asked.

The little gray man stared at him, shaking his head.

"Dear Lord, boy, why don't you just come out and say it, how many of them there are and when you can get them for me. I'm not blind. I've seen lots of figurines like these before. They're all similar."

Tacit thought.

"What if I make you a figurine that you have never seen anywhere else?"

"You can't."

"Then will you believe me?" asked Tacit.

The man hesitated.

"But what will you use to make the cast?" he wanted to know. "Where will you get the original?"

"I make them myself, out of clay and wax."

"God knows you're lying, kid."

Tacit reached for the two apostles, but the dealer wouldn't let him have them. "They can stay here until you come back," he said.

"No," said Tacit. "I'm not doing business with you as long as you think I'm a thief. Where you get your other things from is none of my business, but you're not getting anything from me until I've proven to you I'm no thief."

Tacit took the figurines, rolled them up in the towel again and put them in his pocket.

The little man looked completely perplexed by Tacit's decisiveness.

"There's hardly anyone who can craft sculptures like that nowadays," he assured him, following Tacit back through the corridor. "You could be a rich man if what you are saying is true," he said, almost whispering.

"You can be the judge when I come back," said Tacit. "Since you won't take my word for it."

The decision to make something that the second-hand dealer didn't see every day took the form of a female centaur already on Tacit's walk home. That little dusty man needed to be shaken up, and the most startling pictures Tacit had seen were the centaur pictures that Teacher Melin had. To make it especially obvious that the figure wasn't run-of-the-mill, he bestowed four arms on the woman instead of two. And the effect on the blacksmith was marvelous, in any case.

"Out here in the country," the dealer had said in his most derisive tone of voice. Farmerboy. That's what he thought. Tacit felt offended. He was no farmer and would never be one.

He was a blacksmith, even though he hadn't yet completed his apprenticeship.

It wasn't until he saw the blacksmith's big fists lose their grip on the female centaur at the filing bench, as if the figurine had been on fire, that he understood there might also be a difference between blacksmiths. And more than ever he realized that this little figure with four arms and horse's legs was the key to what he had inside himself—a special kind of blacksmith.

A Survivor

H e was lying on the floor.

And he hadn't as much as attempted to cover himself. He could easily have gotten his overcoat or Granny's knitted blanket up on the bed if he had reached out his arm. But he just lay there, old and scrawny and bare.

This was the second time.

At least his fever had passed. He just couldn't support himself on his bad leg. Tacit hadn't thought it would happen again. He hadn't given it even one thought the whole time he was standing there with the horse, patting it, letting it snatch Granny's dry ryebread crusts with its long crooked teeth. It always took things with its teeth.

And all the while the old man had been just lying in here on the floor without saying anything, without calling out. It wasn't until Tacit had opened the door to the inner room and saw him lying there in front of the bed ....

At first he thought the old man was dead.

But then he noticed his eyes, angry and hateful. The pupils were large, black and wild, but he didn't say a word, didn't move. He just lay there, hating.

Tacit put the pot of food down just inside the door.

"Why didn't you call for me?"

He looked questioningly at the old man to see if maybe there was something wrong. Why didn't he say something? Only his eyes under the reddish bushy brow showed any sign of life. His lips were pressed together to a thin line in the unkempt beard. Tacit bent down and carefully slipped an arm under his haggard body.

"You sure take your time, don't you?" Ælgar said suddenly.

Tacit laid him up in the bed quickly.

"What do you mean?"

"You've been out there with that horse for half an hour."

"Why didn't you say something?"

"Don't you think I know that it's the horse you come for and not me?"

He gave no resistance when Tacit lifted him up. The first time, when he had a fever, he had screamed and struck out.

"I came with your food."

"That's just an excuse. You stayed out there with the horse, and I could just lie here the whole time."

"You could have said something."

"It's cold lying on the floor."

"You could have put something over you." Tacit was annoyed, but he didn't say anything about the wool sweater that still lay untouched on the chair where he had laid it several days before. That would just make things worse.

"Why don't you stay in the bed?" he said instead.

Tacit positioned Ælgar's legs and bunched up the bedding under his broken knee.

"Why do you have to get up? I put a bucket right here."

"I'll rot if I lie here."

"But I said I would come."

"Right, and in the meantime I can just lie here and die on the floor."

"You could just have stayed in bed."

"Don't you think I know you don't care. Nobody cares what happens to me."

"It sure was a hell of a lot of trouble pulling you out of that peat pit. You forget that."

"You could have just left me there. No one asked you to do anything."

"It sure would have been easier. Then it would all be over. But what about the horse? Should it just die of starvation?"

"The old man's eyes flared up in his haggard face.

"I would have drowned her," he hissed.

"Ingelin?"

"I would have drowned both of us."

Tacit could tell by his voice that he meant it, and Ælgar shut his eyes as if in pain.

"Does your knee hurt?" Tacit asked quietly.

"It's your fault."

Tacit sighed.

"You could have just left me alone. You're always so damned meddling."

"The horse came and got me. Ingelin didn't want to die, and I couldn't just let you lie there."

"That bitch—she kicked my knee and broke it. I'll never be able to walk again. What did you have to pull me out for?"

Tacit wondered if it was the knee that made him so bad-tempered, or if he always had been like that. It was almost impossible to satisfy him with anything.

"And then here I get to lie here on the floor freezing for hours," the old man continued irately.

"Why don't you put on the wool sweater?" asked Tacit.

"Charity," sneered the old man. "Your rejects are good enough for me."

"It's not a reject."

"Then what is it?"

"It's the best one I had. I'm sharing it with you."

"Alms for the poor. No one has ever given me anything but charity—and a kick. All my life I've been kicked. And now I'm lying here helpless."

"Granny says that you can stay with us."

The old man twisted his mouth in disgust.

"She means it," assured Tacit.

"Charity. Only charity. It's too late for that.In all the years I've lived here no one has ever worried about how I was or how I got food—or if I ate at all. None of you could care less about me—ever. A wool sweater doesn't change that."

"If I couldn't care less," said Tacit, "then I wouldn't come."

"It's just because you want my horse."

"No it's not," said Tacit, feeling anger rise inside him. What was he making such a blasted stink about?

"Of course it is," maintained the old man maliciously.

"You don't know what you're talking about," answered Tacit, turning towards the pot.

"I don't even know if she's still here," continued the old man.

"Who?"

"Ingelin."

Tacit spun around, staring angrily at the man in the bed.

"You don't know if Ingelin is here?"

He clenched his fists by his sides.

"How could I know?"

"Are you accusing me of stealing your horse?"

"In any case I haven't seen her since you trapped me in here."

"I haven't trapped you."

"Then what have you done?"

"Do you want me to drag you outside?"

"It's like being shut in."

"The door is open—all the time."

"What good is that to me? How do I know when it's open?"

"Is it maybe my fault you can't walk on your leg?"

"You're the one who pulled me out."

"And you think I did it to get the horse?"

"If there still *is* a horse here ...."

The man stared from his bed, contemptuously challenging Tacit. Tacit struggled to suppress his anger.

"You old devil ... you always make everything look so rotten."

"Everything *is* rotten."

"If you wanted to see your damned nag, why didn't you say so?"

"I didn't say I wanted to see any horse. I give up possession of her. She's not here any more."

Tacit tore open the door to the front room and grabbed the yellow horse by the mane.

"Come on ... get in there ... you have to visit the sick," he ordered.

The horse resisted, not wanting to be forced through the narrow door. It put its ears back and dug in its hooves.

"Get in there when I tell you to!"

Tacit was not going to let it get off so easily. He squeezed its nostrils until it gave a moan.

"Treat her right, now," directed the old man from his bed.

"Who? What are you talking about?"

Tacit didn't so much as turn his head towards him.

"The horse, you idiot. Ingelin."

"She's not here," said Tacit. "What are you yelling about? Why should you care when it's not even her."

The yellow horse rumbled in onto the wood floor with every sign of being ill-at-ease in this unfamiliar place. Tacit pulled it all the way over to the bed. It turned its head away from the smell of the bed.

"Can you see her now?" asked Tacit. "Are you sure you can get a glimpse of her, or do you still think I stole your damned livestock?"

The invalid didn't look at the horse, and he didn't lift his hand to pat it. He looked past it, almost without even letting it into his field of vision. But Tacit could tell by the flare of his nostrils that he was enjoying inhaling the smell of horsehide.

Tacit let go, and the yellow horse immediately fled, and not just back to the room where it had been. It continued out through the next door to the farmyard.

He let it go.

Without a word he picked up the pot of food and walked over to the kitchen to warm it up a little. If only he knew why the old man always made such a big stink about everything. Charity ....

He lifted off the stove top covers and went into the shed for kindling. The stove was in bad shape, everything was, here in the house. And no one was doing anything to stop the continual decay. He could at least mortar new firebricks into place, so there wouldn't be a fire. All that was left were the naked iron plates.

Tacit smacked the pot down in the hole and stood watching how the smoke seeped out through all the seams in the stove before settling under the flaking ceiling, like it always did. He started to cough and went back to Ælgar's room.

"Why don't you fix the stove?" he asked. "It leaks."

"There's no bricks in it," Ælgar informed him.

"You could just mortar some in," replied Tacit. "It's dangerous not to have any. Then you could use it in the winter ... and sleep out there."

"I don't have any firebricks. They disintegrated."

"I can get you some."

"It's not my house."

He sounded dismissive, but Tacit didn't give up so easily.

"It's the least you could do for being able to live here," he said.

Ælgar looked at him intently and thoughtfully. Then he said, "Well, I don't live here."

"You don't?"

"This is not living."

"You could move to the kitchen," tempted Tacit. "And have heat. It must get awfully cold here in this room in the winter."

"No one in this parish has frozen as much as I have. When it gets unbearable I go and lay in the hay with Ingelin."

"I could help you," said Tacit, looking out in the farmyard to see if there were smoke coming out of the chimney.

"I can't move into a farm that's not mine."

"But here you are. No one else lives here."

"You need self-respect to live in a farmhouse."

"It's in bad shape anyway."

"People don't notice me so much back here. There's less presumption in taking over an outbuilding, but you wouldn't understand that. It's easier to survive."

"Survive?"

"It's easier to tolerate doing it at the level of a servant. You don't know what it means to have to survive, to be forced to survive."

Standing there, Tacit decided that he would line the stove with new bricks.

"No one else in this parish ever had to try and survive," continued Ælgar angrily. "They just live. They don't have to think about anything."

"I'll bring some bricks with me tomorrow and do it," said Tacit.

The old man didn't respond and Tacit immediately took that as consent. But when he returned the next day the bed was empty. The sight hit Tacit like a blow to his forehead. Had he left? But he couldn't walk on that leg, and he had been too weak to stay upright on only one.

And the horse ... where was the horse?

Tacit rushed around in the stables and out on the grassy slope, but there was no one to be seen.

Could it be that someone came and helped move him?

Or had the old man himself crawled up and over the hills, clutching the long grass with his hands, his broken leg dragging behind. And with the horse following him. Not driven out by water, but by fear. The fear of being noticed and moved to an institution.

Or had the crazy guy drowned himself ... again. But how could he have gotten up on the horse with that leg?

Tacit raced out through the gate and found fresh tracks in the soft black path through the ravine. He started running. The old man had had the whole day to make progress, and the tracks showed only one direction ... he hadn't come back. How long could a weakened old man with only one good leg keep himself afloat?

Tacit was burdened with an increasingly heavy feeling that the old man had long before sunk to the bottom. And the horse hadn't come back alone either. Was he really going to find it floating in the black water with a swollen stomach and a foreleg and a hind leg jutting aimlessly through the water's surface?

But the trail did not turn towards the peat pits. It continued past the place where it had turned last time, and Tacit started running again. He saw that the trail turned down towards the beach. But what could Ælgar do on the beach with a bad leg?

At a bend in the trail he caught sight of the man and the horse farther ahead, with their backs to him, still on their way down ... and this late in the day. Tacit stopped as if he had run into an obstacle.

The old man swung his body along between two crutches and only touched the ground with his good leg. The horse followed slowly behind with its muzzle at the man's sleeve. His old coarse coat flapped heavily with his movements.

The horse turned its head and looked back, recognized Tacit, and stopped. Ælgar turned around on his crutches with a gruff expression.

"What do you want?"

Tacit advanced towards them hesitantly. He didn't want to say that he thought the old man was going to drown himself.

"Where are you going?" he said instead.

"What business if that of yours?"

"I have those bricks."

"I didn't ask you for any bricks."

"I know, but yesterday you were laying on the floor and you couldn't go anywhere. Why didn't you stay there?"

"What makes you think you get to decide what I do?"

The old man hung between the crutches that weren't even crutches, just two pitchforks with the forks pointing up. His eyes had sunken even more than when Tacit first had met him.

"I am used to taking care of myself," he said.

"I came by with your food," said Tacit feebly.

"I didn't ask for any food," was the sharp response.

And Tacit felt the man's hatred for everything lash out through his rejection.

"You are not going to decide what I'm going to eat and where I'm going to live ... or who I am."

Tacit was just about to turn and leave, when he caught sight of his wool sweater, sticking up through the neck inside the long coat. A jolt of of gladness rushed through him, and he quickly averted his gaze, so the old man wouldn't notice that he had seen it.

So he had put it on.

"I'm going down to the beach," said Tacit, starting to walk down the path. The horse walked along, grazing, but Tacit made a point of not talking to it or patting it. The old man turned around suspiciously and started hobbling along with his crutches. Evidently he was going to the beach as well.

"Do you go fishing?" Tacit asked quietly.

"Not with this leg."

"No, but otherwise?"

"There's nowhere I'm allowed. I have a trap out near the mouth of the creek. I haven't emptied it in a long time."

Tacit didn't offer to help him empty it. He didn't offer to help with anything. It was better that way.

Not even when it became apparent that the creek had flooded in the meantime and the trap, partly broken and covered with mud, had been thrown onto dry land. Ælgar poked suspiciously at it with the shaft of one pitchfork. It would have to be repaired before it could be used again.

Tacit didn't say he would repair it. He took comfort in the fact that Granny's good food was in the pot back at the farm. Even though Ælgar didn't get any fish today, he wasn't going to go hungry.

The old man leered over at him as if he knew what he was thinking. Then he started walking away from the mouth of the creek along the beach where a couple of tar-stained rowboats were pulled up on the sand. There were several people living nearby who fished to make ends meet. Ælgar sat down with difficulty to rest against the railing of the first boat. It wasn't easy to trudge along in sand and seaweed with only one leg. And Tacit sat down calmly next to him, turning his head to look out over the water, just like the old man was doing. A weak sea breeze carried the ocean air, and it smelled of tar, salt and half-rotted seaweed. No one said anything for a long while, and the yellow horse walked around on its own, sniffing and blowing in the sand.

Tacit realized that it was better to sit quietly together, instead of carping at one another. He would have liked to have asked if the old man were tired, but he didn't. And when Ælgar later got up, hobbled down to the water's edge, and started laboriously collecting mussels, Tacit followed and did the same.

The old man put the thick closed shellfish into his coat's deep pockets. Tacit filled a bailing bucket from one of the boats.

"What are you doing that for?" asked Ælgar, leering at him.

"There's enough room for two servings in the big iron pot in the kitchen."

"You're going to cause a ruckus if you take the bailing bucket from that pram," warned the old man.

"I'll bring it right back," answered Tacit. "I don't have any good pockets."

"Then put them in mine."

Tacit emptied the filled pail into the one pocket and kept collecting. Ælgar was the one who decided when they had gathered enough. And it was Ælgar who washed the mussels out in the stone trough while Tacit lit the stove and then cleaned plaster and fallen pieces of brick out of the heavy iron pot before filling it with water.

The stove smoked terribly, and Tacit thought about the firebricks he had left out in the farmyard. One day he would mortar them in, but not today. He had to wait and let the things that happened today settle, both in the old man and in himself. It was the wool sweater. It was because the old man had put it on.

"We should have schnapps with this," remarked Tacit,

when Ælgar plopped the mussels into the pot and warmth began to spread around the room.

"Schnapps," said the old man, sprinkling a gray powder down into the pot on the opened shells. "Not something you can just find somewhere."

"What's that stuff?" asked Tacit, pointing to what was left in the old man's hand.

"Salt ... "

"It doesn't look like salt."

"It's more valuable than gold."

"It doesn't cost much at a store."

"I made it myself."

Tacit looked doubtful.

"Salt is something you buy."

"Everything is something you buy," said the old man crossly, "until the day you have no money and no way to get any. Then you don't buy things. You go without, or you make it yourself."

"Out of what?"

"Seawater. I cook seawater every night on the beach during the summer."

"And schnapps?"

The old man sadly shook his head. They sat on opposite sides of the open stove, picking mussels from their shells with the tip of a knife, and sticking them burning hot into their mouths. The red light from the stove fell across the floor.

"Next time we'll have schnapps with them," promised Tacit, slurping down the mussels.

The old man flared up. He hadn't asked for schnapps.

"Otherwise I won't have your salt," said Tacit. "And besides, it's good for your knee."

They continued eating in silence. It was a big pot. Granny didn't have one any bigger, except for the copper kettle. It had most likely come from the people who had left the farm way back then.

Over by the door sat Granny's pot with the potatoes and gravy. They didn't touch it.

THE CHIMNEY WATCH

L ate one afternoon at the end of October, a rider galloped to the entrance of the smithy and pulled up his horse. Tacit lifted his head. Regular farmers would never ride like that on a routine errand, not that fast. Gravel and pebbles rattled against the open smithy door when the rider turned to a stop, and the unusual forcefulness made Tacit drop his work and go outside into the foggy autumn weather. The smell of freshly-turned soil wafted in from the fields, but this was not a plowing farmer who needed a horse shod.

It was old Ælgar from the Water Farm.

Tacit stopped short, astounded at seeing him. The old man had never shown himself before in broad daylight where other people were around. And now here he sat with wild eyes on the back of a lathered horse, here in front of the smithy where anyone could see him. It was unbelievable. There must be something wrong at the farm.

The old man stared intensely at Tacit trying to speak. His beard trembled and his hand flailed in the air.

"What is it?" asked Tacit, starting to loosen his leather apron behind his back.

"You have to come," the old man blurted out, pointing at Tacit.

The blacksmith appeared in the door behind them to hear what was going on, but stopped abruptly at the sight of the strange old man. Slowly he realized that he had seen the man before. He glanced at the yellow horse's hooves which were still unshod.

"What's going on?" asked Tacit, disturbed by Ælgar's appearance. He passed his apron back to the blacksmith.

Ælgar stared at him with terrifying eyes but couldn't explain. "You have to come," he repeated, turning the horse so his stiff right leg pointed the way. Tacit grabbed a corner of the blanket on the horse's back with his hand and started running, while the old man dug his left heel into the yellow horse's side.

Strangely confused, the blacksmith remained standing in the door with the leather apron in his hand. What was all that about? Why didn't they say why they had to run off?

While he ran, Tacit wondered if the Water Farm was on fire, and in his imagination he saw it as a huge flaming blaze. The entire hollow in which it stood was a gigantic fire pit. But there was no smoke.

He slowed down a bit to ask, but Ælgar was focussed on riding. The old man's distraught eyes looked straight ahead, onward. Time was of the essence.

And then Granny's tale about the water rising struck Tacit's imagination. The water that came out of the ground and didn't run away, but flowed out over the edge of the trough, through the farmyard and through the floors of the house. That was a long time ago, but it did happen, and no one could be sure that it would never happen again. The image of people escaping up over the hillside followed by their cows, the cows' necks outstretched because they were being pulled. Could they be right, all the people who said that it would happen again? Not just that there would be water in the farmyard like there was every year during the spring thaw, but that it would enter the house, flowing over the floor, into the rooms, and into the barn?

He turned his head towards the old man and asked.

"Did the water come back?"

He had to shout, but he shouted gently. Where would Ælgar go if the water flooded his room?

The old man turned his face and stared at him with a terrifying expression, a fearful look that must have been how he had appeared when he had committed the murder. The same tortured and wild expression, the same eyes –

"It happened when I picked her up. It wasn't me, it wasn't my fault...."

His voice was like his face, and his beard was turned back over his shoulder. Tacit didn't understand. Who was he talking about? A chill flowed out between his skin and his clothes at the thought of what could have happened.

"It happened when I picked her up," repeated the old man.

What happened? Who was he talking about? Who did he lift up?

"Water. It started running out of her."

The panic in Ælgar's distorted, raised voice was passed on to Tacit.

What water? Who is "her"? The yellow horse's hooves thumped on the ground next to his running feet. The old man's stiff leg stuck out on the other side of the horse.

"Who are you talking about?"

"The girl I picked up."

Tacit grabbed him hard by the sleeve.

"She was lying by the roadside," yelled the old man. "I had to sling her up over the horse. I couldn't carry her. And then it happened. It washed down over my arms and kept on coming out. She's going to give birth –"

"Where is she now?"

"It's not my fault. It wasn't me –"

"Where is she?" Tacit shook him.

"In the bed."

It sounded like a superfluous question.

105

"Last time someone gave birth, I had to kill someone," said the old man.

"It wasn't you," said Tacit, knowing what he thought. "It was her."

"What will they do to me if she dies?"

"Do you know her?"

Ælgar looked at Tacit with his strange, ultra-black eyes, and did not answer.

Ingelin, thought Tacit. It will always be her, no matter who it is.

Beside the horse he raced, down the grassy slope to the farm. Ælgar dismounted and hobbled into the front room. Tacit followed, and inside the room lay a woman he didn't know. Her belly rose high up over the bed. She yelled when she saw them and rolled over on her side, doubled up and moaning in pain.

"Go get Granny," blurted Tacit without looking at the old man.

"Me?"

"You can see how she is."

"I went to get *you*."

Ælgar was passing off responsibility, now that he was no longer alone with the birthing woman. But he had already done almost more than one could expect of him. And Tacit heard it in his voice. Ælgar had ridden into the life that had cast him out; he had shown himself in broad daylight, admitted that he existed. What more could one ask of him?

"You have to get Granny," said Tacit. "She knows what you're supposed to do."

"You can take my horse," replied Ælgar.

But Tacit didn't dare leave the old man alone with the birthing woman. Who could say what could happen now after what he had already done?

"Hurry up, would you?" he said.

Ælgar stared right through Tacit with his wild disturbed eyes and didn't move.

"Otherwise I'll leave," threatened Tacit. "And tell Granny to bring everything she needs for a birth."

The old man bowed his shoulders under the weight of the unavoidable.

"But I already –" he mumbled.

"Hurry up, dammit," shouted Tacit, pushing him out the door and over to the horse, helping him up.

The yellow horse started walking all on its own, and Tacit gave it a little slap on its rear to speed it up.

"Where am I going to put her?" complained the old man before he had even gotten to the gate. It was as if he only just realized that he was going to bring back an old woman.

Tacit lifted his arm and watched him disappear. That side of the bargain he was sure Granny would take care of. If only the old man would hurry. He didn't want to be alone with the woman in there any longer than necessary. He went in and looked at her.

She lay with her eyes closed, awaiting the next contraction. Who was she? Not from their parish. Tacit had never seen her before. How did she happen to be lying by their roadside. Where was she from? She didn't seem like one of those wayfarers who had no place to live. She had on normal clothing.

He went over and sat in the chair by the door. She opened her eyes without moving.

"I sent for Granny," he said quietly.

A shock jolted through the woman, and she raised up on her elbows with a frightened expression, as if she were on the run from something. A second later she bent over double with a moan and laid back on the bed again.

"Where are you from," he asked quietly when the contraction had passed.

She told him. Somewhere so far away that he knew almost nothing about it. So how did she make it here?

"He threw me out. They told him that the child wasn't his, and he threw me out and locked the door. That was three days ago."

Tacit sat there, not knowing what to say. For three days she had been wandering the roads in that condition.

"Where are you going?"

She shook her head.

"Where do your parents live?"

"I can't go home. I can never go home again. They won't take me."

"So, is it true?"

"Yes."

Tacit waited while another contraction came and passed.

"Did you put on water to boil?" she asked suddenly.

"Water?" Tacit looked at her uncomprehending. "Why water?"

"We're going to need a lot of water," she said to herself. "Hot water."

"Why don't you go do it?" she yelled, cradling her stomach in her arms. "Why did you bring me here, then? What are you going to do to me? Why didn't you leave me alone?"

"Don't worry, Granny will be here soon," responded Tacit, feebly defending himself.

"Granny." She mocked the word. "Don't you realize that I'm going to have a baby and that it's coming now?"

Tacit didn't know how he made it to the kitchen, only that he was there, and that he ought to light the stove fast. The covers clattered from his hands, and the ash rose in clouds as he loaded kindling and wood into the stove. He didn't have time to clean it out first. Then he filled the big cast iron pot out at the spring. The water sloshed ice-cold over his hands when he carried it in and set the round burden on the stove. It would take a long time before it would get warm. He lit a clump of dried straw and stuck it in through the stove lid, watching the smoke seep out through the seams. Coughing, he waited for the whoosh to tell him that there was a draft in the chimney.

He brought in more firewood, then walked back to see how the woman in the room was. She was doing worse, nodding her head back and forth in the straw, and clutching the bed edge until her knuckles were white.

And he was alone with her. What if the baby started coming? What if it came now? Where would he put it? And what was he supposed to do with the water? He cursed Ælgar because he was taking so long. Why was he dallying? Why couldn't he get here faster with Granny?

He scampered back to the kitchen and loaded in some more wood, felt the water. "Hot," she had said. It wasn't hot. It wasn't warm at all, not yet. He filled the stove to the top with firewood, pushing in one piece after the other, listening to the flames thundering beneath the ice cold pot and disappearing into the chimney. The sound of fire soothed him for a moment, but as soon as he was back in the room, he was overwhelmed again by confusion and anxiety. The contractions were coming more quickly now, and the woman intermittently tossed and turned in the bed.

Tacit couldn't bear staying in the room and he didn't know what else to do but to keep loading the stove. The stovetop was glowing red in the deepening darkness, and Ælgar hadn't arrived with Granny yet.

He felt the water. Small bubbles were just starting to loosen and float up from the bottom, but it wasn't warm enough. It wasn't really warm at all yet, even though it was unbearably hot now in the dilapidated kitchen. He would have to wait some more.

Finally a wagon rumbled in through the gate and he dashed out and lifted the little old lady down onto the ground before she had even gotten up from her seat, packed in among a jumble of pails, pans and all kinds of bundles.

Tacit pulled her towards the door despite her protests. She wanted her things, too.

"Of course, of course," he said, pushing her in front of him into the room. He could get all that for her.

When he came back out, Ælgar was standing upright in the wagon yelling and waving his arms, pointing up in the sky. Tacit didn't listen to him, but gathered up the bundles and carried them inside. It wasn't until he was finished that he took a moment to see what the old man was trying to show him.

Up through one decrepit chimney on the farmhouse, a yellow plume of fire waved hungrily.

Tacit's hands sunk defeatedly at his sides while he stared at the fire.

It was burning.

The chimney was on fire. The stove. It was that damned stove. He sprinted across the farmyard into the kitchen just in time to see old Ælgar tipping the water from the pot down into the red, glowing stove, which started to boom, shake and spray water so violently it rattled the walls.

"Are you insane?" Tacit exclaimed.

Tacit kicked the stove door closed, trying to keep it shut with his foot while a cloud of steam filled the room. Still the boiling water seeped out of the warped covers and leaky plates, and Tacit had to remove his foot to keep from getting burned.

Then the whole black hot mess streamed across the floor.

Tacit could have cried. He could have screamed and yelled and stamped on the ground at the sight of it. It was all his water. What was he going to do now?

He cursed loudly and unequivocally at the idiot who without thinking dumped out all his good water.

The old man turned around angrily in the mud on his stiff leg.

"You're the insane one. Maybe you noticed the chimney's on fire? You lit it like a fool!"

"You could have used something besides that water!" sputtered Tacit.

"Do you want it to spread?"

"Want what to spread?"

They were furious with one another, both of them unbalanced because a child was about to be born.

"The fire!" sneered Ælgar.

"That was the water she was supposed to use!"

"But there's no bricks in that stove!" The old man shook his head deprecatingly and full of contempt. "It was completely glowing red!"

"It's burning in the chimney," said Tacit, "not down here. What are they going to use to wash the baby?"

"Don't you care if the whole building comes crashing down on us?"

"Is that going to stop it—by dumping water all over the floor—and *that* water—you could have gotten more!"

Using the poker, Tacit started irately emptying the half-burnt, dripping wet pieces of wood out of the burning hot stove. With an angry tug he pulled out the ash drawer so it spilled. The floor was awash with hot water, now mixed with chunks of ash and charcoal.

"You know that chimney leaks."

Ælgar stood upright, preaching at Tacit, with his feet under water and his head in a cloud of steam, which was having trouble escaping. Meanwhile Tacit, fuming, walked over to the henhouse, collected more wood and started building a new fire. He knew that everything leaked and that the chimney was broken, but what did that matter now? He wasn't going to start patching them now, not with her lying over there.

"It's rotten as hell," he hissed, jamming the new firewood down into the wet stove, "and it's your fault that it hasn't been patched in all the time you've lived here."

Ælgar searched for something to say, something hard and evil to defend himself. His beard quivered, but no sounds came from his mouth. The injustice filled too much space. He sloshed over to a kitchen chair and sat down, heavily.

"But when it's already on fire," he almost pleaded, when Tacit lit a dry clump of straw. "It's totally crazy to light the stove ... and like that."

"If you can use the stove then so can I," replied Tacit, placing the filled pot back into the largest ring. Then he figured he'd better go see about Granny.

The old man sat on the decrepit chair shaking his head over such foolishness."Ridiculous ... when the soot is already on fire."

It was almost dark outside when Tacit walked carefully into the first room with the horse. It was quiet in the room at the bed. He stood still for a second listening. He couldn't really tell what kind of quiet it was, but it probably wasn't a good idea to bother them, so he snuck out again and went back.Up at the roof the yellow flame waved calmly.

Tacit hadn't lit the stove as hot this time. It was as if it weren't as necessary, now that Granny was here. The stove door was closed and the chair where Ælgar had been sitting was empty, but the hatch to the attic over the stairs was open. Tacit found the old man up by the chimney, standing there splashing water on the surrounding wood frame with an old whitewashing brush. The fire gleamed through cracks in the hot chimney, and sharp red tongues of flame intermittently flicked out through the holes.

For a while neither of them said a word. Not before Tacit went down with the empty bucket and refilled it out at the spring. The stairs to the attic were narrow and steep and difficult for an old man with a stiff knee. Down in the kitchen he heard the firewood collapse in the stove when he walked by. He let it be. No one had told him the water had to boil.

"Who is she?" the old man asked Tacit quietly when he returned.

"She's not from around here," answered Tacit, telling where she was from and how long she had been on the road.

Ælgar momentarily forgot the lifted brush, and water from it started running down his sleeve.

"But why? And like that? Where was she going?"

"He threw her out," said Tacit, observing the old man's face in the weak reddish glow of a crack.

The old man's eyes grew watchful.

"Someone told him the child wasn't his," continued Tacit. "She had no place to go."

A pained expression of aversion spread across the old man's face, and there was silence between them for a long while, except for the splashing of water on the hot stones followed by the smell of soot.

A wail from outside reached them in the darkness. It was from the barn. They both stopped, frozen where they stood, listening without breathing. It was the baby they heard, crying. Their relief sputtered and sizzled alongside the hot chimney. Now there was a baby in that room. The woman had released her burden and Granny was with her. The old man splashed water on the underside of the roof where it had begun smoking, and he told Tacit where there was another bucket he could use to get more water. The chimney was heating the attic like an oven, but neither of them spoke about going to sleep. They knew they would be there all night.

"It sure is strange," said Ælgar much later.

"What's strange?" asked Tacit.

"Her over there. Why would she end up here?"

Tacit didn't answer. It was quiet in the attic for a while.

Then Ælgar asked, "Where did you say you threw those firebricks?"

Cecil Bødker (born 1927) is one of contemporary Denmark's most highly awarded and prolific female authors. She has written 59 books including poetry, novels for children and adults, short stories and plays. Best known for her young-adult fiction books, in 1976 she received the international Hans Christian Andersen Medal for Writing for her lasting contribution to children's literature. In 1998 she was awarded the Grand Prize of the Danish Academy, the highest honor awarded to an author in Denmark, for her body of work.

Pushcart-nominated literary translator and poet **Michael Goldman** taught himself Danish on a pig farm in Denmark over 30 years ago to help him win the heart of a lovely Danish girl. Over 90 of Goldman's translations of poetry and prose have appeared in more than 35 literary journals such as Rattle, World Literature Today, and International Poetry Review. His other translated books include: *Farming Dreams* by Knud Sørensen (Spuyten Duyvil, 2016) and *Selected Poems of Benny Andersen* (Norvik Press, 2017). He lives in Florence, Mass. www.hammerandhorn.net

Made in the USA
Columbia, SC
27 November 2017